Barbara Cartland, the wo...
novelist, who is also an histori...
cal speaker and television pe...
370 books and sold over 370 million over the world.

She has also had many historical works published and has written four autobiographies as well as the biographies of her mother and that of her brother, Ronald Cartland, who was the first Member of Parliament to be killed in the last war. This book has a preface by Sir Winston Churchill and has just been republished with an introduction by Sir Arthur Bryant.

Love at the Helm, a recent novel, was written with the help and inspiration of the late Admiral of the Fleet, Earl Mountbatten of Burma. This is being sold for the Mountbatten Memorial Trust.

Miss Cartland in 1978 sang an Album of Love Songs with the Royal Philharmonic Orchestra.

In 1976, by writing twenty-one books, she broke the world record and has continued for the following seven years with 24, 20, 23, 24, 24, 25 and 22. In The *Guinness Book of Records* she is listed as the world's top-selling author.

In private life Barbara Cartland, who is a Dame of Grace of the Order of St. John of Jerusalem, Chairman of the St. John Council in Hertfordshire and Deputy President of the St. John Ambulance Brigade, has fought for better conditions and salaries for Midwives and Nurses.

She has championed the cause for old people, had the law altered regarding gypsies and founded the first Romany Gypsy camp in the world.

Barbara Cartland is deeply interested in Vitamin therapy, and is President of the National Association for Health.

Her designs 'Decorating with Love' are being sold all over the USA and the National Home Fashions League made her, in 1981, 'Woman of Achievement'.

Barbara Cartland's book, *Getting Older Growing Younger*, and her cookery book, *The Romance of Food*, have been published in the United Kingdom, the USA and in other parts of the world.

For other titles by Barbara Cartland please see page 144.

BARBARA CARTLAND

ALONE AND AFRAID

Pan Original
Pan Books London and Sydney

First published 1985 by Pan Books Ltd,
Cavaye Place, London SW10 9PG
9 8 7 6 5 4 3 2 1
© Cartland Promotions 1985
ISBN 0 330 28749 4
Photoset by Parker Typesetting Service, Leicester
Printed and bound in Great Britain by
Collins, Glasgow

Author's note

Illegitimacy up until quite recently was a stigma which isolated the unfortunate victim from other people. Unless they had the patronage and help of some aristocrat or Royalty as in the case of William IV's ten children by Mrs. Jordan, they were insulted and hounded all through their lives.

I remember during the last War the Lady-in-Waiting to an exiled and a deposed Queen telling me tearfully she had been born out of wedlock and that she had not dared to accompany Her Majesty to Buckingham Palace without the permission of the King.

In villages the local bastards were cruelly abused and sneered at by other children and were never allowed to forget that they should 'never have been born'.

Yet traditionally 'love children' are beautiful, clever and naturally, like the handsome, fascinating Duke of Monmouth, rebellious.

In this outspoken age it has recently been revealed in a biography that the most beautiful woman of the century was not the daughter of the Duke whose name she bore, but the result of an *affaire de coeur*.

Chapter One
1895

The Marquis of Elkesley picked up the diamond necklace and looked at it closely.

The stones were good quality, but not very large, and before he said anything he glanced at the diamond bracelet he had already chosen and had had set on one side by the Jeweller.

The Marquis was exceedingly generous to the women whom he favoured, and he had promised the bracelet to his mistress, Millie Mervin, after a fiery and satisfying night.

Then he felt he must be fair to the beautiful Countess of Sandford on her birthday.

He had a slight suspicion that she had had a birthday only six months ago, but as she was exceedingly lovely and had surrendered herself to his insistence after a not very arduous chase, he felt she deserved the necklace.

She had in fact mentioned quite casually that she had seen it in the Jeweller's window, and that it resembled one worn by the Princess of Wales.

The Marquis with a twinkle in his eye knew it was a hint that that was what she really wanted for her birthday.

He was used to women taking it for granted that he should give them astronomically expensive presents, as well as paying for anything else that caught their fancy.

At the same time, those who knew him were well aware that he disliked more than anything else being imposed upon, or cheated over the smallest item, even a postage stamp.

"It is all very well, Adamson," he said now, "but I do not think you have reduced this necklace as much as I expected. After all, I have bought the bracelet!"

"I'm very grateful for Your Lordship's patronage," the

Jeweller answered, "but I assure you I'm making practically no profit at all on these items!"

The Marquis laughed.

"Really Adamson, you cannot expect me to believe that. I agree you are entitled to a good profit, but not an abnormal one!"

"I assure Your Lordship my profit isn't abnormal. To be honest, I barely cover expenses."

The elderly man spoke with a note of bitterness in his voice which made the Marquis look at him in surprise.

And yet he had the feeling he was telling the truth.

"How is that possible?" he asked.

"It is possible, M'Lord, because of the high commission I have to pay on anything Your Lordship purchases."

"Commission?" the Marquis asked puzzled.

As if he realised he had made a mistake Mr. Adamson said:

"Excuse me, M'Lord. Forget I said that."

The Marquis put the necklace back in its velvet-lined box and sat back in his chair.

He was a very handsome man and he was also very intelligent. Many women had said that he had penetrating eyes which seemed to look deep into their hearts.

Now there was silence while the Marquis looked fixedly at the Jeweller before he said:

"I want an explanation of what you have just said."

"I apologise, M'Lord. It was a mistake."

"I think that is untrue," the Marquis persisted. "To whom do you pay commission on my purchases?"

The Jeweller looked uncomfortable and embarrassed.

Then with his eyes downcast he moved the trays away from him as if he was too nervous to keep still.

"Tell me," the Marquis insisted, "or I shall walk out of your shop and never come back!"

The Jeweller drew in his breath. Then he said:

"The Countess of Sandford asks for twenty per cent of the cost of anything that is bought for her and she expects me to hand it to her in cash."

The Marquis stiffened.

He could hardly believe that what he was hearing was true although he had often suspected that Ladies of Quality were as avaricious and grasping as any prostitute.

However never until this moment had he been able to substantiate his suspicion.

His lips were pressed in a hard line before he asked:

"Anyone else?"

"Mr. Norman, your secretary, M'Lord, expects five per cent of any purchase Your Lordship makes!"

Now there was a spark of anger in the Marquis's dark eyes and when he spoke again his voice was slow and calm, but at the same time hard.

"I will not take the necklace, Adamson," he said, "but I shall feel under an obligation to buy the next piece of jewellery I require from you. Give me the bracelet, and there will be no question of your paying my secretary or anybody else commission on it!"

"I thank Your Lordship!"

The Jeweller rose hastily from the table at which he had been sitting, and picking up the bracelet took it to an inner office to place it in the leather box and have it wrapped up and sealed.

The Marquis sat where he had left him, keeping his anger under control.

At the same time he was furious at the clever way in which he had been, in effect, robbed both by his secretary and by his current mistress in the social world.

He was in fact less angry with the Countess of Sandford than with himself for not having read her character and for taking her – to put it bluntly 'at her face value'.

Her husband was not a very wealthy man, but they were comfortably off, and could afford to keep a large house in the country, as well as their London house in Park Street.

The Countess was expensively gowned by the best dressmakers and she had already a collection of fine jewellery which was a matter of envy among many of her rivals in Society.

'It is just avarice that makes her want more,' the Marquis thought.

He despised himself for having nearly been beguiled into buying a necklace which would have cost him far more than he usually spent on such a present, and with which at the same time, she would have made a comfortable sum of money for herself.

'I thought I was a judge of character,' he told himself bitterly.

Then he had to admit that like most men he had been taken in by a beautiful face and had not looked deeply into what lay beneath it.

The Jeweller came back from the inner sanctum carrying the parcel in his hand.

The Marquis took it from him and said:

"I am grateful to you, Adamson, for telling me the truth. You shall not suffer for this, and I hope that you will always be as honest with me in the future as you have been today."

"I only hope, M'Lord, I've not caused any trouble," Mr. Adamson said.

The Marquis did not reply and as he left the shop and walked into Bond Street, the Jeweller watched him with a worried expression on his old face.

The Marquis's Chaise, which he drove himself, drawn by two fine horses, was waiting outside in charge of a cockaded, high-hatted groom.

He handed the reins over to the Marquis and jumped up onto the small seat behind even as the horses had started to move.

The Marquis was scowling as he drove out of Bond Street into Bruton Street, and from there into Berkeley Square.

He was wondering how he could tell Lily Sandford in words that would sting like a whip exactly what he thought of her behaviour.

This problem occupied his mind until he arrived back at his large and impressive house in Park Lane.

It had been built by his great-grandfather, and looking out over Hyde Park it had a grandeur of its own which was enhanced by a Ball-Room and Picture Gallery at the back which opened onto a garden.

The Marquis however was not for the moment concerned with his possessions, and passed without noticing them the fine statues which stood in the Entrance Hall.

He handed his hat to one of the four footmen in attendance and as the Butler hurried towards him he said:

"Send Mr. Norman to me, Jenkins! I will be in the Library."

"Very good, M'Lord."

The Marquis went into the Library and sat down at the flat-topped desk on which almost every item from the blotter to the pen-cleaner was embellished with his coat of arms in gold.

The Marquis's family was an ancient one, and many portraits of his Elke ancestors hung on the walls in his house in Park Lane, and even more in Elke Castle in Buckinghamshire.

The present Marquis bore many of the facial characteristics of his forebears: a long straight nose, a square, determined chin, and a high forehead which in every generation denoted brains.

There had been Elkes at the Court of every Reigning Monarch since the time of Henry VIII, and Generals and Admirals of the same name had made their contribution to the history of England.

The door opened and Mr. Norman, a rather furtive-looking man who was not yet forty, came into the room.

As the Marquis looked at him he realised it had been a mistake to appoint him in the first place.

He had however been very pre-occupied with other matters when his previous secretary, who had also served his father, had grown too old and too ill to carry out his duties.

He had therefore appointed the man who had worked under him as his assistant for two years, because he at least was familiar with the running of his houses and estates.

Now he blamed himself for not taking more trouble in placing in so important a position a man who should in his dealings be as blameless as Caesar's wife.

"You sent for me, M'Lord?" Mr. Norman asked.

The Marquis looked his secretary up and down in a manner which was extremely intimidating before he said:

"I want a list immediately of every tradesman and every shopkeeper from whom you have taken commission since you have been in my employment!"

His secretary went very pale and the Marquis continued:

"I am instructing my Accountants to go over the books. You are dismissed from today without a reference!"

His secretary did not speak. He merely went whiter than before as the Marquis finished:

"I have nothing further to say to you. I am only ashamed that anybody in my employment who has an example to set to people beneath him should behave as you have done!"

He got up from his chair as he spoke and walked away towards the window.

For a moment the secretary stood looking at his back and his lips moved as if he would make a plea or perhaps a protest on his own behalf.

Then as if he knew it was utterly hopeless he went from the room, closing the door behind him.

The Marquis returned to his desk, wrote a letter to his Accountant and another to his Solicitors, a firm whom he knew he could trust, then rang the bell.

Jenkins the Butler came hurrying into the Library.

"Have these notes delivered Jenkins, and tell Henson to pack my clothes. I am leaving immediately after luncheon for Paris."

"I will do that, M'Lord."

There was not a flicker of surprise on his face at the orders he had been given, for the Marquis was always unpredictable and his servants were used to his suddenly leaving for the country or going abroad.

Or equally suddenly giving large parties without any warning.

"Do you wish Mr. Wrightson to make the arrangements for Your Lordship?" Jenkins asked.

"Of course!" the Marquis replied. "Tell him I will cross the Channel by Steamer and not use The *Sea Horse* which is now on its way to the Mediterranean."

"I understand, M'Lord."

Jenkins left the Library and the Marquis sat back in his

chair, drumming with his fingers on the desk – a habit he had picked up from the Prince of Wales and which showed he was still in a bad temper.

He knew however that his decision to go to Paris was a wise one. First it would save the trouble of having to explain everything he required to a new secretary.

Secondly, it would save him from having what would undoubtedly be an unpleasant scene with Lily Sandford when he told her what he thought about her.

It would be far more dignified and in a way a far subtler punishment if she did not hear from him, and he simply ignored her birthday tomorrow.

He had planned, knowing that her husband was to be away tonight, that they should dine together.

This meant that when he arrived at her house dinner would be served in her candle-lit *Boudoir,* and they would both be acutely aware that her bedroom with its big bed and soft silk curtains was next door.

He had intended to wait until midnight, and then when he knew that she would be wearing little else he would place the diamond necklace round her neck and wait for her to express her gratitude in the obviously appropriate manner.

'Now she will be disappointed!' he thought savagely.

He remembered the bracelet he had put down on the desk when he went into the Library.

It was quite in order for the gentlemen who were the close friends of the Prince of Wales not only to pursue the Beauties who decorated the parties at Marlborough House like elegant swans on a very expensive lake but also to set up in discreet little houses in St. John's Wood, mistresses who would amuse them when they were satiated with the formality of the Court and social circles.

The Marquis had recently taken under his protection one of the alluring Gaiety Girls.

George Edwardes the brilliant showman of his time, had made his Gaiety Girls very different from anything that had been seen on the stage before.

Not only were they in most cases far better educated and

13

far more attractive, but 'The Guv'nor', as they called him, dressed them as if they were Princesses.

Their underwear was trimmed with real lace, and their spectacular gowns left the audiences at the Gaiety Theatre applauding wildly every evening.

Millie Mervin was a newcomer to the ranks of the Gaiety Girls.

The Marquis had noticed her almost the first evening she appeared, and had met her afterwards at a supper-party given by one of his friends.

This of course had taken place at Romano's, where the most famous of the Gaiety Girls, like Connie Gilchrist, had balls of flowers suspended over their favourite tables.

Millie Mervin, which was a name the Marquis thought had been skilfully chosen, was not only very pretty, but she was also vivacious and witty, and kept him amused in a way no Society Beauty was able to do.

She was also shrewd enough to realise that the Marquis was a 'catch' that any Gaiety Girl would be thrilled to hook, and had therefore not hesitated when he had offered her his protection.

It pleased him when it was obvious that his friends were envious that as usual he had got there first!

The house in which he installed her was small but decorated in excellent taste, and when he visited her there the food, by his arrangement was cooked to his liking, and his favourite brands of claret and champagne were waiting for him at exactly the right temperature.

Every night that he was not obliged to be at Marlborough House in attendance on the Prince or a guest of one of the great Political hostesses, the Marquis sat in his own box at the Gaiety.

After the show was over he took Millie out to supper.

He felt that she had earned the bracelet he had bought for her, and he therefore wrote a note saying he must be away from London for a short while, and addressed it to her at the house in St. John's Wood.

He left the note and the bracelet on the desk, and walking from the Library went towards the Dining-Room where he knew luncheon would be waiting for him.

Because he was a keen athlete, when he was at home luncheon was always a sparse meal, very different from the enormously heavy dinners that he was expected to consume at every house in which he was a guest.

It consisted usually of cold meat and salad.

The Butler and two footmen waited on him, and when he had finished eating in silence and drinking only a small glass of a dry white wine, he said as he rose:

"Is the carriage at the door?"

"Yes, M'Lord!"

It was typical that the Marquis asked no more questions.

Having 'set the wheels in motion', he knew that his clothes would have been packed, his valet would already have gone on ahead to Victoria Station, and his Courier would have reserved a carriage for him.

* * *

Only when England was left behind and he was out of sight of the White Cliffs of Dover did the Marquis feel the anger which had consumed him begin to evaporate.

'I will enjoy myself in Paris,' he thought, 'with women who are true to their calling.'

What he was actually thinking was that the women of Paris were famous all over the world for adhering to a code of behaviour that was as strictly laid down as if it was a law.

It was their professional objective to extract every franc they could from their admirers who ranged from Kings, Potentates and Noblemen of every country in the world down to Bankers and Businessmen who were rich enough to afford such luxuries.

But they also kept to the rules and never attempted to step out of their own class and milieu.

The Marquis had often been amused if when escorting some famous Actress or a Courtesan he met his Social hostess of the night before, and she had looked through him with vacant eyes.

The social barriers were very high and firm, and there was no climbing over them or under them. This made life, he thought, very much more simple.

Because of this he never for one moment had visualised that a social Beauty like the Countess of Sandford would attempt to behave in a manner which he might have expected from Millie, although he was prepared to bet that it had never crossed her mind.

'Paris is where I can forget that I have been defrauded and made to look a fool at least in my own eyes,' he thought.

As he stepped onto French soil he felt some faint stirrings of excitement as if he was going to find something new and original.

The Marquis's house, first off Avenue des Champs Élysées, was always kept in readiness for him at any moment, even without prior warning.

His Major Domo had however received a telegram in advance of his arrival and the red carpet was down over the steps, and the flunkeys in the hall looked alert and smart.

"It is delightful to see you back, *Monsieur*," the Major Domo murmured as the Marquis arrived. "A number of Your Lordship's friends have been enquiring daily if you were here."

The Marquis knew this was not surprising, since the Season in London was coming to an end and before he left for the country he often spent a week or so in Paris to enjoy the racing.

He remembered with pleasure there would be a Race-Meeting at Longchamps in two days' time.

As he looked at the flowers in the garden outside the windows and smelt what he thought of as the fragrance of Paris, he was glad that he had left London.

It was also a satisfaction to think that Lily at this moment would be wondering with some anxiety why she had not heard from him.

He had spent a comfortable night in the *wagon-lit* and although it was still early in the morning, he did not feel in the least fatigued, but rather exhilarated by Paris and the amusements which were waiting for him.

He went upstairs to his large bedroom where the windows overlooked the garden and in the distance he could see through the trees a glimpse of the Seine.

A bath was waiting for him, and he did not hurry, but soaked in the almost cold water.

He dressed himself with the fastidiousness of a man who was not obsessed by his clothes, but liked them to be as perfect as everything else around him.

He poured himself a glass of champagne, then went into one of the smaller Salons where he usually sat when he was alone.

There were pictures on the wall by famous artists which were part of the family collection.

He had added to them rather daringly two Impressionist pictures which his friends had laughed at, calling them useless daubs by absinthe-soaked ne'er-do-wells, which would never be worth more than the canvas on which they were painted.

But the Marquis, who had other ideas, did not feel inclined to argue about it.

He simply bought what attracted him and added to the Elke collection begun by his ancestors and now famous throughout the world of art.

There were several notes on his blotter, which he knew had been left by those who had called seeking to learn when he was coming to Paris, while his Factotum had dealt with the accounts and other uninteresting items of his correspondence.

One envelope in blue smelt of gardenias, and the Marquis opened it with a faint smile on his lips as he recognised the fragrance.

It was, as he expected, from Celeste Lozere who was one of the most notorious *Demi-Mondaines* in the whole of Paris, and the most acclaimed for her beauty.

The Marquis had had a passionate affaire with her two years ago, but she had remained strangely enough a firm friend.

Now he recalled how entrancing she was and how she had gained her reputation not only for her looks but also for her expertise in the *sciences d'amour*.

The note was written in her clear hand-writing that was

very unlike the illiterate scrawls of some of her rivals.

She wrote:

"Mon cher:

I suspect you will soon be in Paris and it is important that I see you immediately. I have something to impart which concerns you, and you alone, and I therefore beg you to get in touch with me.

> *I remain, as always,*
> *Yours with affection,*
> *Celeste."*

The Marquis looked at what she had written with surprise.

He could not imagine what she had to tell him, but he was quite certain she would not have written as she had without a very good reason for it.

He looked at the date on top of the note and realised it had been written only two days ago.

"I wonder what she wants?" he asked himself.

He read the letter again, thinking perhaps there was a clue in it that he had missed.

Then he told himself if nothing else Celeste had made him curious, and he certainly would visit her immediately. After all, having only just arrived in Paris, he had no other plans.

He looked at the clock and knew that though it was nearly noon Celeste would not yet be up unless she had a luncheon appointment, which was unlikely.

She always received her callers in the morning, looking exquisitely beautiful in a Louis XIV bed, carved and gilded, with muslin curtains falling from a corola of cupids which was fixed to the ceiling.

It was a bed in which the Marquis had followed a succession of distinguished lovers, and he was sure that none of them had been disappointed as Celeste had always been all things to all men.

He ordered his carriage, and when it arrived he thought the horses seemed a little over-fresh as if they had not been properly exercised.

He therefore spoke sharply to his grooms, who assured

him that they did in fact gallop the horses every morning in the Bois. Nevertheless he told himself he would make up for any deficiency on that account while he was in Paris.

The sun was shining and although it was hot there was a pleasant breeze blowing from the river.

The carriage was open and the Marquis appreciated the beauty of the trees, the children playing beneath them, and the old man selling balloons as he had done ever since he could remember.

There were the fountains in the Place de la Concorde throwing their water, iridescent and glittering with rainbows, towards the sky.

It was all very familiar and very attractive, and by the time the horses stopped outside Celeste's house in the Rue de Faubourg St. Honoré the Marquis knew the last vestige of his ill-humour had been swept away.

It was typical, he thought with a smile, that she should have installed herself in a street which also contained the British Embassy and other houses owned by French Grandees.

One servant opened the door and recognising the Marquis greeted him effusively.

"It's good to see you back, *Monsieur*," he said, "*Madame* will be delighted! She was saying only a short while ago that she was hoping you would soon return to Paris."

"Well, I am here," the Marquis said good-humouredly, 'so inform *Madame* that I wish to see her!"

"She will be delighted, yes, delighted!" the man murmured as he went upstairs ahead of the Marquis to where, as he had guessed, Celeste was still in bed.

She was wearing a crisp muslin dressing-jacket with the sleeves interwoven with blue ribbon, her dark hair falling on either side of her pointed face.

She looked very alluring as she gave a cry of joy and held out her arms to the Marquis.

"*Mon brave!* You are here! she exclaimed. "This is an answer to my prayers. I cannot express in words how pleased I am to see you!"

"Then why try?" the Marquis asked.

He raised both her hands to his lips, then as she put her arms round his neck he kissed her lips.

She smelt, as she always had, of gardenias, and he remembered how the exotic perfume had lingered on his own skin long after he had left her.

Then he sat down in the chair by the bed, crossed his legs and said:

"I opened your note as soon as I arrived, which was only this morning. What has happened? You have made me curious."

"I have a problem which only you can solve," Celeste replied.

"I cannot believe there are not a dozen gentlemen ready and willing to solve any problem that worries your pretty head," the Marquis smiled.

"That is where you are wrong!" Celeste exclaimed.

At that moment the Butler came in with a glass of champagne which he handed to the Marquis.

As he did so Celeste patted the lace-trimmed silk pillows behind her head and was very conscious, the Marquis knew, of how attractive she looked.

Her dark eyes slanted up slightly at the corners, and her red lips curved in a particularly inviting way which most men found irresistible.

The Marquis sipped his champagne. Then he said:

"I am listening."

"I really want to talk about you," Celeste said, "but this has to be said, and you have to help me."

"I will certainly do my best," the Marquis answered, "but I make no promises."

Celeste paused, then she said:

"You must have heard of, even if you never met him, your relative Gerald Elke."

Whatever else the Marquis had expected, it was not this, and he stared at Celeste in astonishment before he said:

"Gerald Elke? Do you mean my father's cousin who behaved in a disgraceful way many years ago?"

"Yes, that is the man I mean."

"Good Heavens!" the Marquis exclaimed. "I have not thought of Gerald in years. Anyway, he is dead!"

"Yes, he died seven years ago to be exact!"

"I do not understand. Whatever has Gerald Elke got to do with you? And what is this problem concerning him which you say only I can solve?"

As he spoke he was thinking that Gerald Elke, whom he had met on several occasions when he was a boy, had been one of the most handsome and the most raffish of the family.

He had by all accounts exceeded even the accepted quota of reprehensible love-affairs that were expected of a young Man-about-Town.

He had thereby gained a reputation which had shocked the family, who were very conscious in their various positions at Court of the Queen's sense of propriety and disapproval of anything immoral.

Thinking back, the Marquis remembered that it must have been about twenty years ago that his cousin Gerald Elke had run away with the beautiful wife of one of Her Majesty's Court Officials.

It took him a second or two to remember her name, then he recalled it had been Blyton, and Lady Blyton had been a Lady-in-Waiting to the Queen.

The scandal had hit the family like bomb explosion, and the Queen had been outraged at such behaviour on the part of one of her Ladies.

Lord Blyton, who was very much older than his wife, had been obliged to retire to the country.

He had not even considered petitioning for a divorce, since that would have brought the scandal to the knowledge of the ordinary public.

Instead he had merely vented his wrath on the Elke family, who indeed were as appalled as he was.

Gerald Elke and Lady Blyton had however behaved better than might have been expected, for they disappeared.

Looking back the Marquis could remember vaguely his mother and various other members of the family asking if anything had been heard of Gerald, and the answer had always been a shake of the head.

However badly a gentleman behaved it was always possible that, if he was penitent, he would be taken back into the bosom of the family.

But Lady Blyton was never mentioned, because a lady who had become in their eyes a 'scarlet woman' would never in any circumstances be forgiven.

Aloud the Marquis said:

"Of course I remember now, although I was only a boy at the time, what a scandal Gerald caused, and I can only ask what has happened now to resurrect him?"

"Not him but his daughter."

"Daughter!"

The Marquis's exclamation rang out like a pistol-shot.

"Yes, his daughter," Celeste replied, "and quite frankly, *Mon Cher,* I have not the slightest idea what to do about her."

"I do not understand," the Marquis said. "First, I had no idea that Gerald had a child, and secondly what has happened to her mother?"

"Her mother is also now dead, and that is why she has come to me."

"I still do not understand."

"I am not surprised," Celeste said with a smile. "Even you with your quick brain would find it hard to believe the story which might have come out of the *Arabian Nights*."

"Why not begin at the beginning?" the Marquis suggested as he took another sip of champagne.

"It all started when Kitrina, that is her name, her mother and your cousin Gerald were all blissfully happy together."

"Where were they living?" the Marquis interrupted.

"According to Kitrina, in many places. They went to Africa, and she talks of Cairo, Algiers, Casablanca, and strange places in the desert as you and I might talk of Chantilly or St. Cloud."

"Go on."

"When Kitrina was ten years of age, her father died."

"I had no idea of that," the Marquis murmured.

"They were in Morocco at the time, so that is not surprising. According to Kitrina, her mother was desperately unhappy, in fact all she wanted was to die too."

"Somewhat disconcerting for a child of ten!" the Marquis murmured dryly.

"It must indeed have been frightening for her," Celeste said softly.

"Then what happened?"

"In Morocco they met a Frenchman on his way to be Governor of Senegal, the *Comte* de Villeneuve."

The Marquis smiled.

"So that solved one problem."

"Not completely," Celeste said, "because being French he was of course already married."

The Marquis thought cynically that should not have worried Clare Blyton, who had been 'living in sin' ever since running away with his cousin.

He did not interrupt however, and Celeste continued:

"When the *Comte* asked Kitrina's mother to go with him to Dakar – his wife, needless to say, was remaining behind in France – Kitrina was put into a Convent School."

"Where?"

"In Florence, and there she remained until a month ago."

The Marquis raised his eyebrows as he asked:

"Are you saying the child has not seen her mother for seven years?"

"Only occasionally. Apparently she would not have Kitrina with her while she was living with the *Comte*, and although I understand she wrote to her every week, Kitrina spent her holidays with friends, or at the Convent with the Nuns."

"It seems extraordinary to me," the Marquis commented, "but go on."

"Well, Kitrina had an urgent message from Algiers to say that her Mother was dying."

The Marquis was listening intently as Celeste continued:

"It was arranged for somebody to take her to Algiers where she found her Mother was already dead."

23

The Marquis made a murmur of sympathy and Celeste went on:

"She finds it hard to talk about it but according to what she told me, the *Comte* had died only a week or so earlier, having contracted one of those pestilential fevers which are so prevalent in Africa. After his death her Mother developed the same fever and the Doctor said there was no chance of saving her."

"So what happened? And how do you come into this?"

"That is what is so strange," Celeste admitted. "I had been a close friend of André, the *Comte* de Villeneuve. In fact, he was my first protector when I came to Paris."

The Marquis smiled and almost added:

"There have been a large number since!"

However he did not interrupt but merely waited to hear more of the story.

"He always had a certain tenderness for me," Celeste went on, "and every year he remembered the anniversary of our first meeting and when he first made love to me."

There was a faint smile on her lips as she said:

"He used to send me presents, sometimes money, sometimes jewels, but he never forgot."

There was a sadness in her voice which made the Marquis remember, almost as if somebody was quoting Byron's lines aloud:

"In her first passion woman loves her lover,
In all the others all she loves is love."

"Kitrina told me," Celeste went on, "that she went through all the correspondence she could find in the Villa, because she wondered frantically what she should do, and where she could go. Then in a desk she found my letters to André which I had written year after year, thanking him for his gifts."

"So she came to Paris!"

"She saved what was worth saving in the Villa, although apparently the servants had run away, taking

24

with them all they could of any value. However she did bring away with her a number of small items which had belonged to her father."

Celeste ticked them off on her fingers as she went on:

"Cuff-links, a gold watch, a cigar-case, a travelling-clock, a set of pearl studs, which had been locked in a safe. As they all bore your family crest, I knew whom I had to approach if I was to help Kitrina."

There was silence before the Marquis said:

"Do you think that is wise? After all, as she is illegitimate she is not really entitled to call herself by my name. Unless she is unattractive, which I can hardly believe considering how good-looking her father and mother both were, she should perhaps follow the lead of many lovely women in Paris. And who better to instruct her than you?"

Celeste gave a little laugh.

"That is exactly what I thought you might say, and I would agree with you but for two things."

"What are they?"

"First, I do not think Kitrina knows that her father and mother were not married. Secondly, when you have seen her, I shall be surprised if you give me the same advice."

"She is too plain to play the part?" the Marquis asked sharply.

"Perhaps you should judge for yourself."

"Very well," he said resignedly, "but actually I think it would be a mistake for me to be involved in all this. Gerald cut off all connection with the family when he eloped in that disgraceful manner with the Queen's Lady-in-Waiting, and unless you have already said a great deal about me to Kitrina, it would be wisest if she were not aware of my existence."

"She was aware of it long before she came to me."

"How do you know?"

"Apparently her father often talked of the family home which you now occupy, and I suppose because in a way he was homesick, whenever he came across an English newspaper he searched the Court Circular for any references to your family, and would read them out to Kitrina."

The Marquis thought considering Gerald's behaviour that had been an extremely stupid thing to do.

What was the point of making his child aware of relations by blood who never if they could help it, would acknowledge her existence?

At the same time he told himself he could not be so churlish as to refuse to help Celeste in what she considered a very real problem.

There was silence for a moment before he said:

"Very well, Celeste, you have forced my hand. While I cannot promise to do anything except perhaps help this girl financially, I will see her and, if you agree, try to persuade her to throw herself on your mercy and learn from the most acclaimed expert arts which only Paris can provide so gracefully."

As he spoke there was a smile on Celeste's lips that he did not understand.

There was an expression in her eyes which told him, although he could not think why, that she was amused.

He wondered if she thought it funny that he, who had managed with some difficulty to remain a bachelor, should suddenly be saddled with a family problem.

Because the idea irritated him the Marquis said:

"Where do you want me to see this girl?"

"Certainly not here in my bedroom, which I think would shock her," Celeste replied. "Go downstairs to the Sitting-Room, and I will tell my maid to send her to you."

"Very well," the Marquis agreed, "I will come back afterwards to tell you what I have decided you should do, and how I am prepared to help."

He went from the room as he spoke.

As he went down the stairs he thought this was the very last problem he had expected to find waiting for him in Paris, and with Celeste of all people.

"Damn Gerald!" he swore to himself as he opened the door of Celeste's very attractive Sitting-Room. "He was a confounded nuisance when he was alive and now he is a nuisance after he is dead! How dare he bring a child into the world in such circumstances?"

With no one in the room the answer his question, the Marquis stood stiffly in front of the fireplace, waiting for Gerald's illegitimate daughter to join him.

Chapter Two

There was a long wait during which the Marquis had time to think that perhaps Gerald's daughter had done the right thing in coming to Celeste.

After all, he argued to himself, it would be impossible for any member of the family to accept her, considering the circumstances of her birth.

In fact he was quite certain that even if he offered to pay any of his elderly cousins who were extremely hard up, to take her into their home they would refuse.

As he looked back he remembered all too clearly the tremendous sensation there had been after Gerald had run away with the Queen's Lady-in-Waiting.

It had been impossible to prevent the story from circulating, not merely within the Elke family, but also over the whole of London Society.

He was at School at the time, and when even the boys at Eton had teased him about what they had heard from their parents, he remembered then being ashamed of his cousin and thinking that he had defamed the family name.

'If she is attractive,' he told himself, 'there is no reason why she should not, with Celeste's help, become one of the stars of Paris, but I must make it very clear to her that she is not entitled to use our name.'

He recalled that Celeste had referred to her as an 'Elke' and decided that was something he would make quite sure was not permitted in the future.

He felt the whole thing was extremely distasteful and uncomfortable, and it was infuriating that having just escaped from the problems confronting him in London, he should now be confronted by more problems in Paris.

'I will make it clear, absolutely clear that she has no call on the family. If I give her a generous allowance, then in return she must be prepared to forget who she is, and adopt a new name and a new identity.'

He was wondering if Kitrina would resent what he intended to say, and he was scowling as the door opened and someone came in.

For a moment he felt this could not possibly be the girl of whom Celeste had been speaking.

In fact at the other end of the room there appeared to be entering a child, and quite a young child at that.

However, when she came towards him he saw it was in fact a young girl, but she did not look at all as he had expected. In fact she was so lovely that he could only stare at her in astonishment.

Only as she reached him and dropped a curtsy did he find his voice and manage to ask:

"Are you Kitrina?"

"*Madame* Lozere has told me that you are the Marquis of Elkesley and the head of my father's family."

"That is right," the Marquis replied.

"Then I am so thrilled to meet you," Kitrina said, "but I had expected from what Papa told me about you, that you would be very much older than you are."

"Your father would have been speaking of my father," the Marquis replied, "who died seven years ago."

Kitrina gave a deep sigh.

"That is when Papa died . . and I miss him just as if it happened . . yesterday."

She spoke with a little sob in her voice that told the Marquis how much her father had meant to her.

Looking down at her, for she was much smaller than somehow he had expected, he tried to see some resemblance to his cousin.

As if Kitrina was doing the same thing she said:

"In some ways you are like Papa. He too was very handsome, and I think you . . both have the . . family nose."

"That is true."

"And your eyes are like his, except that you were looking cross as I came into the room. Is that because I am a . . nuisance to . . you?"

The ingenuous way in which she spoke made it impossible for the Marquis to say that was indeed the truth, and he could only stare and go on staring.

Never had he imagined that anybody could look like gold, and not be an angel in one of the Bavarian Churches.

Kitrina's hair was the gold of the sun when it first rises over the horizon, her skin was like a translucent pearl, and her eyes, instead of being the rather insipid blue that usually went with such colouring, were the blue of the alpine flowers which the Marquis had seen in Switzerland.

There was too an aura of youth and innocence about her which made him realise exactly why Celeste had sent for him and made no attempt to look after Kitrina herself.

Then as he thought of it he told himself he was being ridiculous.

The child was the result of two people behaving in a disgraceful, immoral manner, upsetting not only two distinguished families, but also the Queen herself.

In a voice which he deliberately made rather crisp and business-like he asked:

"Suppose, Kitrina, you sit down and tell me exactly why you are here and what you intend to do about the future."

She gave him a smile and seated herself on the nearest chair which was an upright one.

He had the feeling that because she was so small her legs looked almost as if they were dangling like a child's, and her feet barely touched the ground.

The very plain gown she wore added to the illusion of her youth, except that the Marquis was aware from the soft curves of her breasts that she was in fact no longer a child, but a young woman.

Nevertheless she clasped her hands together in her lap and said:

"Shall I . . start at the very . . beginning?"

"I think that would be wise," the Marquis agreed as he seated himself in a comfortable armchair. "As you must be aware, I had no idea that you even existed until a few minutes ago."

"Did you find that very . . disconcerting?" she asked unexpectedly.

"As a matter of fact I was extremely surprised!" the Marquis admitted. "I did not even know your father was dead."

"I suppose Mama might have sent a notice to the English newspapers, but when it happened we were in the middle of Africa. Afterwards, when we got back to civilisation, there seemed to be no particular point in telling people that Papa was no longer alive when they had shown no interest in him for twelve years."

She spoke with a touch of resentment in her voice, and the Marquis said:

"As I expect you are aware, your father behaved in a somewhat reprehensible manner which upset all his family and your mother's as well."

He spoke to her as if she was a schoolchild, and to his surprise Kitrina smiled and said:

"I expected you to feel like that. At the same time, it was very, very romantic, and they were so blissfully happy that wherever we lived, even when it was in a tent, everything was filled with love."

She spoke with a rapt note in her voice that made it hard for the Marquis to make any further comments about her father.

Instead he said:

"Suppose you go on with your story?"

"I was born in Africa," Kitrina began. "I can first remember, when I was only four or five years old, riding on camels and sleeping in tents or in Arab villages, where everybody made a fuss of me, so I suppose I was spoilt."

She gave a little laugh as she said:

"The Bedouins always used to think I looked very strange because I was so fair, and some of the tribes thought I would turn out to be a witch!"

She laughed again and it was a very joyous sound.

"Papa said I looked like an angel, which was what he often called me."

The Marquis had thought the same thing, but he made no comment and Kitrina continued:

"We had a wonderful time, and I never remember Papa being cross, except when the camels bit through their ropes and ran away, or when our tent blew over in a sandstorm. Otherwise it always seems to me that for the first ten years of my life, the sun shone every day and Papa and Mama were like the fairy Prince and Princess in a book."

"What do you know about books?" the Marquis interposed. "I cannot imagine you had many lessons in the middle of the desert!"

"That is where you are wrong," Kitrina replied, "Mama used to read to me history books, not only about Africa, but about the world. Papa taught me arithmetic, and, of course, I learnt not only French, and Mama insisted that I had a Parisian accent, but also Arabic and the different dialects of the tribes."

"And you think that will be useful to you now?" the Marquis asked sarcastically.

Kitrina answered him seriously, and putting her head a little on one side, which he found a somewhat fascinating gesture, she said:

"I suppose even in Paris there must be people who want to learn Arabic."

"So you think you might be a teacher?"

"I . . I am not certain," she answered. "At the Convent I learnt enough on every subject to be able to teach children their elementary lessons. But when I suggested that to *Madame* Lozere, she said she was quite sure nobody would engage me as a Governess because I looked so young."

"Did she suggest anything you might do?" the Marquis asked.

"Not really. She said I was a problem and the only person who could solve it would be you."

That was exactly what the Marquis expected and his lips tightened as he went on:

"You have not told me why you went to the Convent."

"After Papa died," Kitrina answered, "Mama and I went to Tangiers where we had bought a small house to stay in between our journeyings into the desert, but Mama was very, very unhappy."

She gave a sigh as she said:

"I think really she wanted to . . die too so that she could . . be with Papa. But for my sake she made an effort, although it was very difficult for her and I knew that she . . cried every . . night."

Kitrina's voice was very soft and despite himself the Marquis felt moved by it.

"Then unexpectedly an old friend of Papa's came to see him, not realising he was dead. His name was the *Comte* de Villeneuve."

The Marquis listened knowing already how the *Comte* came into the story.

"Mama was pleased to see him," Kitrina went on, "because she could talk to him about Papa. Then after he had been in Tangier for a month, Mama told me one day that she had decided I was to go to Florence to be educated."

"And did that please you?"

"Please me?" Kitrina repeated. "I could not . . bear to . . leave Mama. In fact I begged her over and over again to let me . . stay with . . her."

"And what did she reply?" the Marquis asked, knowing the answer.

"She said that the *Comte* had offered to take her with him to Dakar and find her something to do there which would occupy her mind and help her to forget."

The Marquis knew exactly what that was, but he was aware as Kitrina continued, that as a child she had no understanding of what the *Comte* and her mother had planned.

"Mama told me," she was saying, "that I should only be in her way and also she did not think at the time, that Dakar was at all suitable for me. What was more, she said:

" 'Darling, I know you have had a few lessons from Papa and me, but they are not enough. All the Elkes are very clever, and I would hate you to be the exception.' "

There was a cynical twist to the Marquis's lips as he

realised that Lady Blyton had played on the family pride in convincing her daughter that they should be separated.

"Of course," Kitrina said, "I could not refuse after that to do what Mama wanted, so she took me to Florence and left me in charge of the Mother Superior."

"There was no difficulty about your being accepted in the School?"

"No, why should there be?" Kitrina asked. "I think the *Comte* also used his influence, for later I found they would only take a limited number of pupils, so I was in fact very fortunate to be educated there."

"And you stayed there for seven years without seeing your mother?"

"Oh, no!" Kitrina replied. "Of course I saw my mother! She would come from Dakar every year to spend three weeks or a month of the summer holidays with me. She said it was too expensive for me to go all the way to Dakar and back. We therefore stayed in small hotels in the Italian countryside, or over the border in France, and we were very, very . . happy . . together."

The Marquis had been about to ask if the *Comte* was ever with them, then he understood without being told that it was on these occasions that the *Comte* returned to his wife and family, and that was why it was easy for Kitrina's mother to be with her daughter.

"And so you saw your mother once a year."

"Sometimes it was twice," Kitrina said, "but not always. I used to mark off the days on a calendar. When I saw her it was so exciting and so wonderful that it was worth waiting for, and of course we wrote to each other every week."

There was silence until she said:

"Then, just when I was thinking it was time for me to leave the Convent, since I was older than most of the girls there, the Mother Superior had a letter from Dakar asking her to send me out to Algiers immediately because Mama was . . very ill."

She made a sound that was like a sob before she said:

"I could hardly . . believe it! I had heard from Mama only the previous week, telling me all about the things she

34

was doing in Algiers and describing the Villa into which she had moved. She wrote about it so vividly that I felt I could almost see it myself!"

"And you had expected to join her there when you left School?" the Marquis queried.

"Of course," Kitrina answered, "but Mama had not told me yet when I was to leave, although I had asked her several times if I could do so."

"Was she living alone in the Villa when you arrived in Africa?"

"She was . . already . . dead when I . . arrived."

Now Kitrina's voice had deepened and the Marquis could hear the pain in it.

"I . . could not . . believe it was . . true," she went on after a moment. "The Villa was just as she had described it to me . . and she had also sent me some photographs of it . . taken with one of the new cameras. Of course, not being in colour, they did not really depict how . . beautiful it . . all was."

There was a little pause. Then she said:

"The . . beauty of it seemed . . wrong when . . Mama was not . . there to . . enjoy it . . and I was . . alone."

The Marquis heard the tears in her voice and realised she was clutching her fingers so tightly together in her lap that the knuckles showed white.

It struck him that for a young woman Kitrina was very self-controlled, and he felt it was somehow touching that she did not wish to break down in front of him, knowing it would be embarrassing for them both.

He rose to his feet and went to a table in the corner of the room where he knew of old there were always drinks of every sort and description for the gentlemen who called on Celeste.

There was also, he found, a bottle of mineral water and he poured some into a glass and handed it to Kitrina.

"Thank you," she said.

She gave him a wistful little smile and drank half the glass before she set it down beside her.

"It was only after the Doctor who was . . very kind to me

35

. told me he had arranged for Mama to be . . buried and the funeral was over . . that I realised I had . . nowhere to go, and . . nobody to ask what I . . should do."

"You did not think of remaining in Africa?"

She was silent, and he wondered why she did not answer him immediately. Then she said:

"I did think of it . . then . . something h.happened."

"What?"

"A gentleman called to . . see the *Comte*.

"The servants had told me when I arrived that the *Comte* had died in the Villa a week earlier. I suppose he was staying with Mama."

There was silence and then Kitrina looking at the Marquis with a puzzled expression on her face, remarked:

"I did wonder if Mama would not have found it very lonely living in such a large Villa . . and also how she could have afforded to . . keep it up."

The Marquis thought he could have told her, but decided it would be a mistake.

He merely said:

"You were telling me about the gentleman who called to see the *Comte* de Villeneuve."

"Yes . . of course," Kitrina replied, "but . . I am not quite certain whether you would describe him as a . . gentleman . . he was not English . . he was a . . Sheikh."

The way she spoke and the way her eyes looked away from him made the Marquis ask sharply:

"Did this Sheikh upset you?"

"He . . he was a . . horrid man and he . . frightened me."

"In what way?"

"He . . suggested that I should go with him to his Kasbah . . and when I refused . . he would not listen."

Now there was a look of fear in Kitrina's eyes that told the Marquis very clearly that she had been extremely frightened.

The Sheikh had obviously known that her mother had been 'living in sin' with the *Comte* and had assumed that her daughter would accept with alacrity his proposal.

36

He was also aware that with her fair hair and skin she would be the prize in any Arab harem.

"What did you do?" he asked.

"I knew I had to go away, so I made the servants pack up everything I could take with me, and then I boarded the first ship that was leaving Algiers for Marseilles."

"Did you sell the house?"

"I do not know if it is mine to sell. Although I looked through Mama's papers I could find nothing of any importance, except the letters I had written to her from the Convent. She had kept all those."

The Marquis waited, knowing from what Celeste had told him how Kitrina had found her letters to the *Comte.*

"I looked everywhere," Kitrina went on, "hoping to find the deeds of the Villa, or a will if Mama had left one. If she had, it was not there. Then in a desk in another room I found a lot of letters written to the *Comte* from *Madame* Lozere."

"So that was why you came to Paris!"

"I thought she might be able to help me as she knew the *Comte* so well. She also might know if he had given Mama the Villa because she worked for him."

"I understand," the Marquis said, "and I think it was quite a reasonable supposition."

Kitrina gave him a watery little smile.

"But when I arrived four days ago *Madame* Lozere said that you would be more likely to have an answer to the problem of what I should do."

She spoke quite simply and now she looked at the Marquis trustingly, as if she thought he had some magical formula to sweep away all her perplexities.

"You have certainly set me a problem," the Marquis replied, "and you will have to allow me a little time to think of an answer."

"Of course," Kitrina agreed, "but there is one thing I ought to tell you."

"What is that?" the Marquis enquired.

"I am afraid I have . . very little money."

He saw the colour come into her face as she spoke as if

she was ashamed to admit it. Then she said:

"I am sure Mama must have some money in a Bank somewhere . . but there was nothing amongst her papers in the Villa. The only things in the safe were Papa's watch and a travelling-clock, his cuff-links, his gold cigar-case and some pearl studs which he used to wear in his shirt front in the evenings."

She looked at the Marquis a little piteously as she asked:

"I cannot think what can have happened to Mama's jewels unless the servants stole them as they stole other things from the Villa. There were marks on the walls where pictures had hung and mirrors."

"If they could have got into the safe, I imagine they would have taken your father's things as well," the Marquis remarked.

"That is what I thought," Kitrina agreed, "so perhaps Mama had to sell her jewels after she left Dakar and went to Algiers. Anyway, they were not there, nor was there any money."

The Marquis thought for a moment before he said:

"My Lawyers in Paris will be able to find out who owns the Villa, and if when it is sold the money should come to you."

"If you could do that it would be very kind of you," Kitrina said, "but . . I have no wish to be an encumbrance to you in the meantime . . so could you advise me what I can do?"

"I think we can discuss that later," the Marquis replied. "What I am going to suggest now is that you pack your luggage and I will take you from here to my own house near the Champs Élysées."

He was considerably surprised to find himself suggesting this.

At the same time, he knew that it was impossible for him to leave this child, for she was nothing more, in the house of one of the most notorious *Demi-Mondaines* in Paris.

But he could not think on the spur of the moment of anywhere else she could go.

"Are you . . quite sure you . . want me?" Kitrina asked. "Perhaps I shall be in the . . way."

"It may be only for a short time," the Marquis said, "and I

38

expect you are aware that it would be impossible for you to stay alone in an Hotel."

Kitrina looked at him in surprise.

"I thought Hotels were open to anybody who could pay what they asked for their rooms!"

It was an ingenuous remark which told the Marquis again how innocent she was.

"Run and pack your clothes," he said, "I will go to tell *Madame* Lozere I am taking you away with me. I will also thank her for having you here."

Kitrina rose to her feet.

"It will be very exciting to see your house," she said. "Are there any pictures of Papa in it?"

The Marquis shook his head.

"I am afraid not," he said, "but . . ."

He was just about to say that there were pictures of him together with many of the other Elke relatives in the family house in England.

Then he told himself that would be a very foolish thing to say when it was doubtful if Kitrina would ever see them.

"I would like to see a picture of Papa," she said longingly. "It is so sad that cameras were not invented when he was alive . . or if they were . . we did not have one in the desert!"

She laughed as if it was a funny idea, and the Marquis found himself smiling in response.

"I will go to get ready," she said, "and thank you . . thank you very much for being so kind to me. I am sure Papa will be delighted that I am here with the head of the family."

She ran from the room, and only as the Marquis followed her slowly did he realise that she had spoken as if her father knew what was happening.

It seemed that for this strange and unusual girl her father and mother were still alive, even though she could not see them.

It was a subject which he felt was slightly embarrassing.

As he went up the stairs again to Celeste's bedroom on the First Floor he felt that he would have to be very careful

39

in what he said so as : ot to upset or disillusion Kitrina too quickly.

It would all come out in time, of course it would.

He could not remember ever before having met or heard of a young girl who had been incarcerated in a Convent for seven years and then on coming out into the world was completely ignorant of the things that other girls would have learnt from the people they met in the holidays.

Then he wondered whether perhaps her girlish talk and air of innocence were deliberately assumed.

Surely she could not be so stupid when her father and mother were living in sin not to be aware of it, and later not guess that her mother was the mistress of the *Comte* de Villeneuve.

He knocked on the door of Celeste's room and when she called "Come in", he found that she was still in bed, and looking at him with a hint of mischief in her eyes.

"What do you think of Kitrina?" she asked.

The Marquis sat down in the chair by the bed before he answered:

"I have a suspicion she is too good to be true, and all that innocence which matches her appearance is just an act!"

He spoke abruptly and was surprised when Celeste laughed.

"I asked myself the same question, *Mon Cher*," she said, "for I could not believe that in this day and age any girl of nearly eighteen could appear to have stepped down from the clouds of Heaven and have no idea of what the world is really like."

"And what was your conclusion?" the Marquis asked.

"That she is completely and absolutely genuine, and that is why I knew that only you could decide what was to be done about her."

The Marquis was silent and she said:

"I know quite well what you are thinking, that I could find her a very rich Protector and start her off on the primrose path which so many beautiful young girls have found very comfortable and very satisfactory."

Celeste paused. Then she said:

"I am a Catholic, and I know that when I go to Confession I would be remembering – 'whosoever shall offend one of these little ones, it were better for him that a millstone were hanged about his neck'!"

She spoke solemnly. Then as the Marquis laughed she said:

"You may laugh, but no one knows better than I do that it would be morally wrong deliberately to tempt or force a small angel like Kitrina into a life of what the Church calls 'sin'."

"You surprise me, Celeste!" the Marquis remarked dryly.

At the same time he was not really surprised.

Celeste was in many ways different from the other *Demi-Mondaines* he had met, who had no interests above the acquiring of as much money and as many jewels as they could, and were concerned only with their own interest.

He knew Celeste was at the top of her profession because she was intelligent and could talk of other things besides the pleasure of the body.

The Marquis invariably visited her when he was in Paris, even though he no longer desired her as a woman.

"I know exactly what you are saying to me," he said after a moment, "and that is why, although I have no idea what I can do for Kitrina, I am taking her away from here to my own house."

Celeste smiled.

"That is what I hoped you would do. She has come to no harm since she has been with me, but it is difficult to keep her out of sight of my callers and, as you are well aware, if she was seen it would be impossible to stop them from pursuing her."

"I gather there was a man in Algiers who frightened her," the Marquis said. "A Sheikh. Did she mention him to you?"

"I realised something had happened when she said that she was quite happy to have dinner alone in her room when I had guests," Celeste replied. "When I asked her why, she said a little evasively that as she was in mourning for her

41

mother she did not wish to meet any gentlemen."

"Well, there is no chance of her meeting that man again."

"Not if she is with you, but Sheikh Hassan El Abdulla is often in Paris."

The Marquis looked surprised.

"You know him?"

"I have met him," Celeste answered. "He is not a man I would recommend to any fastidious woman, let alone an innocent child like Kitrina!"

"Then she must certainly avoid him," the Marquis agreed.

He felt as he spoke that Paris was the last place for somebody as lovely as Kitrina, who as far as he was concerned, was 'between the devil and the deep blue sea'.

He could not take her to England with him, she was too old to be at School, and certainly too young to look after children or be a teacher, as she had suggested.

Besides, women being what they were, what woman would accept into her house anyone who looked as lovely and unusual as Kitrina?

"I know exactly what you are thinking," Celeste said, "and I have thought of it myself. There is only one thing you can do, *Mon Cher,* and that is to somehow make her acceptable to your family. After all, her father was your relative."

"One of whom I am not at all proud," the Marquis retorted sharply, "and who has been disowned by my entire family."

Celeste flung out her hands in a typically French gesture.

" 'The sins of the fathers shall be visited upon the children'," she quoted. "It is not fair!"

"A lot of things are not fair in life," the Marquis said, "and that is something Kitrina will have to learn sooner or later."

"Then try to make it later," Celeste begged. "She is so young, so pure and untouched. She reminds me of myself when first I left home to come to Paris thinking it was a wonderful place, filled with kind people who would never think of harming me!"

The Marquis had never heard her speak like this before and he asked curiously:

"What happened?"

"I got a job – and I thought I was very lucky – with a French *Duc* and his wife who lived just off the Bois in a very comfortable and luxurious mansion."

"What were your duties?"

Celeste smiled.

"I was a very under-chambermaid."

The Marquis laughed.

"You have never told me that before!"

"It did not last very long," Celeste replied. "The *Comte* de Villeneuve came to stay, and you know the rest of the story."

"A success story," he said, "and you have remained through it all, Celeste, a very understanding, warm and sympathetic woman."

"I like to hear you say that," she smiled, "but I think it was because the *Comte* was a gentle man who taught me a great deal about life as well as helping me to educate myself. Kitrina's mother was very lucky in having him as a lover until he died."

The Marquis was about to reply when there came a knock at the door.

"Who is it?" Celeste asked.

A maid came in.

"*M'mselle* is waiting, *Madame,* to leave, and she asks if she can come to say goodbye to you."

"Yes, of course," Celeste replied. "But first I shall ask *Monsieur* to leave."

The maid closed the door and she held out her hand to the Marquis.

"It is best for her not to see you in here," she said. "As I told you, ever since she came to stay with me I have been remembering what I would have felt when I was her age."

The Marquis rose to his feet.

"Whatever anyone may say about you, Celeste," he said, "you are a good woman and to me a very dear friend."

He kissed her affectionately and Celeste put up her hand to touch his cheek with her long fingers.

"Look after little Kitrina," she said, "and be very, very careful not to let her fall in love with you."

She smiled at the surprise in the Marquis's eyes as she added:

"Too many women have broken their hearts over you, *Mon Brave* and a great many more will do so in the future. Find the child a nice respectable husband, then you can forget about her."

The Marquis laughed and kissed Celeste again.

As he walked to the door she said:

"You laugh, but you are more handsome and more attractive than ever! Come and dine with me one evening. I have a very lovely friend who is longing to meet you."

"As soon as I am free, I shall accept your invitation with pleasure," the Marquis replied.

He opened the door and Celeste added:

"And do not forget to let me know what you are doing about Kitrina."

"No, of course not," he replied.

When he reached the hall he saw a pile of trunks and he had only waited a few minutes before Kitrina came running down the stairs and he knew she had said goodbye to Celeste.

She was looking very lovely, and at the same time still ridiculously young.

She had a small round straw hat on the back of her head which he was sure had been suitable while she was at the Convent, but made her appear even younger than she did already.

She wore a blue bolero over her white gown and there was a blue sash around her waist which tied in a bow at the back, and was the same colour as her eyes.

The Marquis felt she had only to complete the picture with a hoop and she would look like the children playing under the trees in the Champs Élysées.

"Are you expecting me to take all this luggage with us?" he asked as she reached him.

"I am afraid it is rather a lot," Kitrina admitted, "but I could not bear to leave all Mama's clothes behind at the Villa, knowing they would only be stolen and sold in the Bazaar."

She glanced at the trunks before she added:

"Her furs had already gone, and I suspect the servants took those. But I packed up everything else. As I have no money, I though I might be able to alter the gowns and wear them myself."

"A sensible idea," the Marquis approved dryly. "May I suggest now that we drive to my house without encumbering ourselves, and I will send my servants to collect the trunks?"

"That is a good idea," Kitrina smiled.

She got into the open carriage, and when the Marquis sat down beside her and the horses moved off, she slipped her hand into his.

"It is very, very exciting to be with you," she said. "How lucky I am that *Madame* Lozere knew you, and also that you have come to Paris at just the right moment."

The Marquis wished to say that as far as he was concerned it was at the wrong moment.

But he could feel Kitrina's fingers in his and thought it was impossible to say anything that might spoil her obvious happiness.

They drove on and as they reached the Place de la Concorde Kitrina said:

"I was just thinking that it must be Papa and Mama who want you to take care of me, and it was very foolish of me when I found Mama was . . dead to think I was . . alone."

She spoke as if she was really talking to herself, and the Marquis found it impossible to reply.

He merely sat in silence, thinking uncomfortably as her fingers clung to his that it was going to be very difficult to shelve a responsibility that Kitrina was taking for granted.

Chapter Three

As Kitrina finished what was on her plate she said with a little sign of satisfaction:

"Do you always eat such delicious meals?"

The Marquis smiled.

He had realised that the somewhat exotic dinner cooked by his Chef had tempted Kitrina to eat every dish greedily like a child.

He thought it was a long time since he had had a meal with a woman alone who had not played about with her food fastidiously because she was thinking of her figure.

"I am glad you appreciate good food," he replied.

"Of course I do!" Kitrina said. "But I have not enjoyed a meal like this since Mama and I used to go to little Restaurants near wherever we were staying. They were always far better in France than in Italy."

"Tell me about your mother," the Marquis said.

As he spoke he thought it surprising that he should be feeling any interest in Lady Blyton, but in fact he knew nothing about her.

Apart from the fact that everybody had been horrified when she had run away with his cousin, and that she had been acclaimed for her beauty, he had heard little else, perhaps because at the time he had only been a Schoolboy.

Kitrina sat back in her chair.

Then she said in a rapt voice which the Marquis had already heard when she was talking of something which moved her deeply:

"Mama was so beautiful! She was just like all the heroines of history and the Saints of the Church rolled into one."

"That is certainly very generous praise!" he said somewhat sarcastically.

"It is true," Kitrina insisted. "Papa said once that after a man had looked at Mama, it was impossible for him to think that any other woman even existed."

"Are you like her?"

"Not really, and of course I never could be as lovely as she was."

"But your hair is like hers."

"My hair is like Mama's, my eyes are like Papa's, and he always said I had a distinct resemblance to his Elke ancestors. That is why I want to see portraits of them."

The Marquis looked back and thought that perhaps with the exception of a portrait of his great-great-grandmother by Sir Joshua Reynolds, he could not see any particular resemblance to Kitrina.

None of the Elkes as far as he could remember had looked like a small angel, and it was impossible to describe her in any other way.

"What I think was different about Mama from the other ladies Papa had known before he loved her," Kitrina was saying, "was that she was so clever and so amusing."

The Marquis raised his eyebrows.

This was certainly something he had not expected.

"The reason why Mama wanted me to be well-educated," Kitrina went on, "was that she had had a very different education from most girls of her age."

"Why was that?" the Marquis enquired.

"She had three brothers, and before they went to Eton she shared their Tutors with them, and therefore learnt the same things that they did."

The Marquis was surprised.

"Do you mean Latin and Greek?" he asked, remembering what subjects he had learnt when he was young.

"And Mathematics, History and of course Geography," Kitrina added.

Then she went on:

"Mama said it was the Geography lessons which made her long to travel all over the world, and especially to Africa."

"Then it was she who suggested that was where she and your father should go when they . . ."

The Marquis stopped.

He had been about to say; "When they ran away together," but he was not certain whether or not Kitrina was aware that her mother was already married before she caused such a scandal at Court by eloping with his Cousin Gerald.

As if she knew what he was thinking Kitrina looked at him a little shyly and said:

"Mama told me that she and Papa eloped because she not only loved him overwhelmingly, so that nothing else was of any consequence, but also because she was very unhappy."

"How could she be unhappy?" the Marquis asked without thinking. "Did she not hold the important position of Lady-in-Waiting to the Queen, which must have made her the envy of almost every woman in England?"

Kitrina looked at him with a faint air of surprise. Then she said as if she was thinking it out for herself:

"I suppose like most people you think money and possessions and social rank bring happiness, but that is not true."

"How do you know?"

"Because Mama and Papa were completely happy with very little money, often without a roof over their heads, and none of what Papa called 'the glittering baubles of life', for which almost everybody fights and strives."

The Marquis thought that this was a ridiculous statement, and he said:

"Nevertheless those are things which go to make life comfortable and give most sensible people a goal to aim for."

Kitrina put her head a little on one side as she said:

"Do you mean for instance, striving to be Prime Minister, Ambassador or perhaps a General in the Service of the Queen?"

"Exactly!" the Marquis agreed. "Of course for most people, their ambitions may not be so spectacular, but nevertheless it is what makes them work and struggle to attain what is out of reach."

There was a smile on Kitrina's lips as she said:

"Is that what you have done?"

The Marquis was silent for a moment, thinking this was a difficult question to answer. Then he said:

"As you are aware from what your father told you, I am the head of the family because I was my father's son, and he inherited from his father. But because I am in such a position, I do my best to carry on the traditions of the Elke family and to look after those who bear my name."

He thought as he spoke he was getting into rather deep water.

The child questioning him was not entitled to bear his name, although because she was her father's daughter he supposed he would have to do something about her.

"That sounds very grand!" Kitrina said. "But what are you aiming for secretly in yourself? Not with regard to your already vast possessions, but your personality, and of course, your heart?"

It was such a surprising question that the Marquis could only stare at her, thinking that never in his whole life had he been asked anything so unusual.

When he did not reply Kitrina said:

"I expect because you are English you will be too embarrassed to say that you are striving for happiness, which of course would mean . . love."

"I do not believe that is true," the Marquis said sharply. "Certainly it is something I have not formulated even to myself."

"But it is there, of course it is there," Kitrina insisted. "Mama said everybody wanted love, even if they would not admit it, and for some people the choice is very difficult. Others know that nothing material can matter compared to the wonder and glory of loving and being loved."

What she was saying, the Marquis thought, made a lot of sense, but what was so strange was to hear such statements being uttered so positively by a girl who was so young and looked so childlike.

The women who had loved him had always told him that nothing mattered to them except their love for him.

At the same time he was well aware they might not have

been so ardent or so voluble if he had not been so distinguished and so wealthy.

He often wondered to himself how many women in actual fact would have been so profusely and overwhelmingly emotional where he was concerned had he been poor and unimportant.

Now for the first time in his life he asked himself if he had ever met a woman for whom he would have thought it worth sacrificing his social position, or giving up even a tenth of his fortune.

Because he found the conversation had taken an embarrassing turn he said:

"Unless you would like some dessert, why do we not go back to the Salon where it is more comfortable than in this room?"

"That is a good idea!" Kitrina said enthusiastically. "I want to look at your beautiful Sèvres china, and specially the snuff-boxes that you have in a cabinet."

She got up from the table as she spoke and as the Marquis rose to his feet she said:

"I know in England the gentlemen stay in the Dining-Room and drink their port, but as we are in France we can leave the room together."

"I see you have been well taught," the Marquis said without thinking.

"Mama was very insistent that I should have good manners and know how to behave in every country we visited."

She paused for a moment before she said:

"But I have never been to England, so when you take me there I shall have to be very careful not to make mistakes."

The Marquis had no wish to discuss whether or not he should take her to England.

As they walked back towards the Salon he thought what he should really do was to make it quite clear that she was not a member of the Elke family, and he must find her not only somewhere to live, but also a new name.

He could not however bring himself when they were in the Salon to sweep away the expression of happiness on her face as Kitrina exclaimed with delight at everything she saw.

"I know that picture is a Fragonard!" she cried, and before the Marquis could reply was enthusing over a piece of Dresden china, and a moment later over a Louis XIV Commode that was actually a museum piece.

Only when she had been all round the room did she come back to where he was sitting in the armchair watching her, to drop down on the rug at his feet.

"It is all so beautiful," she exclaimed, "and I suppose Elke Castle is even finer! I have never forgotten the things Papa told me about it."

"So he used to talk about it!" the Marquis remarked.

"I think actually he was often homesick for England," Kitrina said, "and when he felt like that he used to put his arms round Mama and say:

" 'Tell me, my darling, that you love me, and that you do not miss the Balls, the pretty gowns, and all that jewellery that used to make you glitter like a Christmas Tree!' "

"What did your mother reply?" the Marquis asked because he was curious.

"Mama used to laugh," Kitrina said, "and say: 'I have everything a woman could want here with you, and when I am in your arms I am enclosed in dreams and the stars overhead glitter far more dazzlingly than any diamond could do!' "

She gave a little sigh.

"Then they would forget I was there until Papa would say:

" 'You must never marry, my poppet, until you are as much in love as your mother and I are. Always remember that nothing else in life is of any importance.' "

"So that is what you are looking for," the Marquis said quietly.

"Of course," Kitrina agreed, "but there is something I want to say to . . you."

"What is that?"

She looked away from him and he thought she was shy. While he waited he wondered what was in her mind.

"*Madame* Lozere said," Kitrina began after a moment, "that because you are head of Papa's family, you are now my Guardian, and I must do whatever you tell me to to do. But please . . promise you will not . . make me marry . . anybody I do not . . love."

The Marquis knew this was a pertinent question because, although she had no idea of it, he was going to find it difficult to find her a husband of any sort.

Because of her looks, a Protector would be easy, but a husband was a very different matter.

The type of man he would consider the right sort of husband for a young girl who was related to him, even if it was, as the servants would say, "on the wrong side of the blanket", would find such a marriage unthinkable.

Furthermore, she would be looked at with contempt by his father, mother, brothers and sisters, and all his other relations.

The Victorian code of propriety as set by the Queen was not only strict, but completely unbending where a woman was concerned.

Had she been a boy, it would have been comparatively easy, the Marquis thought, to take him back to England and persuade the Elke family to accept him as his Ward.

In time the more generous-minded of them would gradually forget his father's misdeeds.

Where a girl was concerned it was very different.

He knew that if he suggested to any of his female relations that they should present her to the Social World, they would think he was deranged.

"We need not consider the question of your marriage yet," he said aloud.

As he spoke he knew he had given Kitrina the answer she wanted.

The smile was back on her lips, illuminating her whole face and making her eyes shine.

"That is what I wanted you to say, but I was afraid that was what you were planning."

"I thought you knew no young men, having been at the Convent all these years," the Marquis said.

Kitrina laughed.

"That is true, and I could hardly marry one of the Priests who instructed us and are of course celibate, or the Music-Teacher who was a very old man with a wife and nine grandchildren."

She laughed again, and the sound seemed to echo round the Salon.

"My difficulty," the Marquis said slowly and, he thought to himself, a little pompously, "is to decide what I shall do with you, Kitrina."

"I can answer that question easily," she replied. "Now that I have met you, I know that I am no longer frightened, as I was at first when *Madame* Lozere said she was sending for you, and I am happy, very happy to be with you."

The Marquis drew in his breath.

"Now listen, Kitrina . . ." he began, but it was too late.

She jumped up from the floor and seeming almost to fly like a small bird across the room she sat down at the piano which stood at the far end of it.

She opened the lid, struck a chord, then started to play a gay and attractive melody which seemed somehow in keeping with her appearance.

The Marquis was aware it was a French Folksong, to which the young people danced at Festivals.

It had a lilt and a tune which lingered in the mind long after the music stopped.

He knew Kitrina was expressing, as she played, her delight at being with him, and although she had not directly so expressed it at being a part of a family.

'I have to tell her the truth!' the Marquis told himself.

Then he thought it would be a mistake to upset her tonight and it would be wisest to wait until tomorrow, when perhaps what he had to say would be easier than it was at the moment.

Kitrina went on to play one of Chopin's Sonatas, and then to the Marquis's surprise a Strauss Waltz.

She played well, and only when she jumped up from the piano-stool to ask: "Did you like that?" did he enquire:

"Where did you learn to play Strauss? I should have

53

thought in a Convent School such frivolities were frowned upon!"

"We all had dancing lessons," Kitrina replied. "It was considered good for our posture and taught us to move gracefully. Moreover all the girls, except me, would have Balls given for them when they left School."

"Did that upset you?"

"Mama used to sigh," Kitrina replied, "and say:

'I wish, darling, I could take you to the sort of Balls which I attended when I was a Débutante. They were very, very glamorous.' "

"And did that make you envious?" the Marquis enquired.

"I thought it would be lovely to go to a Ball," Kitrina admitted. "At the same time, if I had the choice, I would rather have gone adventuring with Papa and Mama. We journeyed across the desert on camels, or rode horses that had Arab blood in them and were, I am sure, faster than anything in your stables!"

She spoke as though she was challenging him and the Marquis said:

"That unfortunately is something we cannot prove, but I presume what you are hoping to do is to ride with me."

"Oh, please let me do that!" Kitrina pleaded. "Mama and I used to hire horses when we were on our holidays together but they were not very good ones, and usually came from Livery Stables, where they were worked too hard and not fed properly."

"If you are to ride in Paris," the Marquis observed, "Then I suppose the first thing I must do is to buy you a riding-habit."

He paused, then he added:

"And I expect you need other clothes."

To his surprise Kitrina hesitated before she said:

"I have not yet had time to look through Mama's clothes. I packed everything very quickly, because I wanted to get away. She was small and slim, as I am, and I expect she had a riding-habit that will fit me. I am sure also that with some small alterations I could wear her gowns."

54

She spoke with a sincerity which told the Marquis she considered this a satisfactory answer to his question.

He knew this was the first time that any woman to whom he had offered a present had ever told him she could make do with what she had.

Only a week ago Millie had presented him with a bill for six extremely expensive gowns which he had thought were worth the money because she looked so pretty in them.

Lily Sandford had been effusively grateful for an ermine cape to wear in the evening which he had thought at the time had cost an exorbitant sum.

Now he knew it was because the Furrier had been obliged to add to it the twenty per cent commission she required in cash.

He must have scowled at the thought for Kitrina gave a little cry and asked:

"What is . . wrong? What have I said that has . . made you . . angry?"

"It is nothing you have said," the Marquis assured her quickly, "just something I was thinking about."

"Then it was not because I appeared . . ungrateful for what you . . suggested?"

"No, of course not."

"I am grateful . . of course I am grateful when you say you will give me a riding-habit and perhaps a gown but I do not want to feel that as a . . poor relation I am an . . encumbrance."

"Is that what you are afraid of being?"

"Yes, of course I am," Kitrina said, "and it is very worrying not to have any money or to know what has happened to Mama's."

She sat down once again at the Marquis's feet and as she looked up at him he saw the bewilderment in her eyes as she asked:

"How could she have paid for that large Villa? Or my School fees and the lovely holidays we spent together in France and Italy?"

The Marquis did not answer and Kitrina went on as if she was talking to herself:

"Of course, as Mama was so clever, I am sure she earned a lot working in Dakar for the *Comte* but she cannot have earned as much as that!"

"When you father died did he leave her no money?" the Marquis enquired.

"I do not really know," Kitrina answered. "Mama was so unhappy and all I could think of was trying to comfort her. I suppose she did not want to talk very much about the future, or what we should do with ourselves."

"I can understand that."

"When she said she was going to work for the *Comte* in Dakar," Kitrina went on, "she seemed happier and although I was miserable at having to leave her and go to Florence, I understood there was nothing else I could do, and it would have been unkind if I had made a fuss."

"Of course," the Marquis agreed, "and you were happy at the Convent?"

"It was strange at first," Kitrina admitted. "The girls used to laugh at me because I knew so little about the things that interested them."

"What sort of things?"

"The Opera, popular music, the French novels they read, although the Nuns disapproved of most of them. And of course they used to talk all the time of their homes, how big their Châteaux were, or their Villas in Italy."

"And you could only talk about a tent in the desert," the Marquis smiled. "That must have been very frustrating!"

Kitrina laughed.

"Actually, I used to talk about the strange feasts to which we had been invited by the Chieftains of the various tribes, and how because they thought Papa was so important, he was always given the sheep's eye as a special treat."

She laughed again and because it was infectious, the Marquis laughed too.

"Did your father eat the eye?" he asked.

"Not if he could help it," Kitrina answered. "He was

very clever in slipping it away with a sleight of hand which he said himself was as good as any Magician's. Or else he would distract the Chieftain's attention so that he was not aware of what he was doing."

"I can see you have had a very different education from that of most young women of your age," the Marquis remarked, "and what do you think it has done for you?"

He was teasing her, but Kitrina took his question seriously.

"I think what it has done first," she replied, "is to make me realise how much more there always is to learn and how I must be receptive to new ideas and new thoughts."

"That is not the answer I expected you to give," the Marquis said. "Now I suggest we go back to where we started: to discuss what you can do in the future, taking into consideration what your education has fitted you for."

"Now you are being unkind," Kitrina complained. "I have already told you that the only way I can make money is by teaching children or perhaps translating English into Arabic, although that is something I have no wish to do."

She spoke quickly, and gave a little shiver as she spoke, and the Marquis asked:

"Why have you no wish to do that?"

Then he knew without Kitrina saying any more that she was thinking of the Sheikh who had frightened her, and was afraid that any Arabs with whom she came in contact might behave in the same manner.

He remembered she had not been in Africa since she was a child of ten until she went to Algiers to find her mother had died before she could arrive.

He could understand that whatever the Sheikh had said or done, it had shocked her to the point where she had no wish to go back.

"I think," he said, "we can discount your knowledge of Arabic. You are now in Europe, and that is where I suspect you will want to live in the future."

"Do you mean on the Continent?" Kitrina questioned. "Oh, no! I would much rather live in England. After all, Papa and Mama were both English, and I know, although I have never been there, that that is where I belong."

She spoke positively as if there could be no possible argument about it, and once again the Marquis was wondering what he should do!

How could he explain to this ignorant child the difficulties involved in what she had suggested?

Because he was tired after spending the previous night in the train, he went up to bed early.

When they reached the First Floor and came first to Kitrina's room which was half-way down the main passage, what was known as the Master Suite at the far end of it, she said:

"Thank you for a lovely, lovely evening. It has been so exciting talking to you, and I feel as if I had stepped back in time and you were Papa because we used to talk to each other in just the same way."

She paused. Then she said:

"I am certain now, although I had forgotten, that your voice is like his."

"I am glad you have been happy," the Marquis said.

"Very happy," Kitrina replied, "and it is very wonderful for me to know you are my Guardian, and I am no longer alone, as I was when I arrived in Paris."

He was well aware than when it was known that she was with him alone in his house in the Champs Élysées, it would either be assumed that she was his mistress, or he would have to explain that she was in fact his Ward, because her father had been his relative.

'If I had any sense,' he told himself, 'I would send her away immediately, and not become more involved than I am already.'

The question was – where could he send her?

She was, he knew, too old to go back to the Convent and anyway, even if they would take her for another term, it would hardly solve the problem for the future.

Her father was dead, her mother was dead.

The way she had been brought up seemed to the Marquis more and more mysterious, and yet he could understand that Lady Blyton was doing the best she could for her daughter.

While she herself was living an immoral life through what

58

must have been sheer necessity, she had obviously had no intention of allowing Kitrina to be aware of it.

It seemed incredible that she had been able to deceive the girl for so many years, and yet the Marquis knew from what he had seen of Kitrina that it had never entered her head that her mother was anything but good.

'Celeste is right,' the Marquis told himself. 'Kitrina does not know that her parents were not married.'

It annoyed him that he should have to be the one to tell her the truth.

He thought it extremely unfair that Gerald, who had apparently had no compunction about hurting other people's feelings, should have extended his selfishness so long after his death in leaving his daughter in ignorance of his outrageous behaviour.

"The whole thing is infuriating!" the Marquis said sharply as his valet left the room.

"Did you speak, M'Lord?" Henson asked.

"It was only talking to myself."

"It's nice to be back in Paris, M'Lord," Henson remarked. "I expect you'll want to go riding soon after breakfast."

He did not wait for the Marquis to reply but went from the bedroom shutting the door behind him.

The Marquis walked to the window, pushed back the curtains and looked out.

There was enough light from the stars to see the garden spread out below the window, and he could smell the fragrance of the flowers.

It was strange for him to be going to bed so early when he knew the lights would be glittering, Bands would be playing, and the two worlds of Paris, the *Monde* and the *Demi-Monde* would both be ready to welcome him.

He was, however, not only tired but worried, and until he had solved the problem of Kitrina he would not be able to enjoy himself.

'Damn Gerald!' he cursed. 'Why can I not have fun like other men and be as irresponsible as they are?'

He knew the answer was that he took his position in life

very seriously, and part of that involved being head of the Elke family and being a father-figure to Kitrina.

He had to protect her and guide her in the way he would protect anybody with the name of Elke.

'But that is not Kitrina's name,' he argued.

Then he knew that he was clutching at straws, and however much he tried to evade the issue, it was something he had to solve, and solve quickly.

* * *

In her bedroom Kitrina was lying awake having said a long and fervent prayer of gratitude because she had found the head of her father's family.

'Forgive me, Papa, for thinking you had forgotten about me,' she said softly, 'and even if you had forgotten, Mama would have reminded you. I am so happy to be with him, and now I am no longer frightened.'

As she lay in bed she remembered how terrifying it had been when the Sheikh had been shown by the old servant into the Sitting-Room where she was sorting through her mother's papers.

He had not announced the caller's name, but merely said there was a gentleman to see the *Comte* de Villeneuve.

Kitrina had risen from the chair in which she had been sitting, and when she had seen a man wearing the Arab head-dress and the inevitable loose cotton garment over Western riding-clothes and polished boots, she had not, in fact, been surprised.

Her mother had told her that while she was in Dakar the *Comte* was in continual consultation with the Arab tribes both in the North and the South.

He had managed in many cases not only to find a solution to their various problems, but to prevent old grievances and insults from causing minor wars.

The man who had just been shown into the room was tall, and Kitrina guessed from his height, his broad shoulders, and his long legs that he belonged to one of the tribes that she knew lived in and around Southern Morocco and were handsome and athletic.

They were also, her mother had said, very much better

educated than some of the other tribes.

She was therefore not surprised when the visitor spoke to her in quite good French.

"I wish to see the *Comte* de Villeneuve."

"Unfortunately, this is impossible," Kitrina replied. "In fact, I only learnt when I arrived that he died a few weeks ago and I expect it was of the same fever which has just killed my mother."

The Sheikh stared at her in surprise. Then he said:

"The *Comte* is dead, and also your mother? My condolence, *Mademoiselle*. It is a very grievous loss."

"Very grievous," Kitrina replied, and found it hard to prevent the tears from coming into her eyes.

There was a little silence, then as if she suddenly remembered that in the East manners were very important, she said:

"Will you sit down, and would you care for some refreshment? A cup of mint tea, perhaps?"

The Sheikh inclined his head.

"That would be very pleasant."

Kitrina called a servant, and as was usual in an Arab country mint tea was on hand, and it arrived in small cups without handles, set in pretty silver holders.

The Sheikh sipped his slowly, his dark eyes looking at Kitrina as he did so, in a way that made her feel somewhat embarrassed. After a few moments he said:

"I think, *Mademoiselle,* I am right in thinking you are the daughter of *Madame* Elke?"

"Yes, I am," Kitrina replied. "And my name is Kitrina."

"And what, *Mademoiselle* Kitrina, do you intend to do now?" he asked. "Will you close the Villa, or will you live here?"

"I have just arrived from my School in Florence," Kitrina replied, "and have not yet made a decision, but I do not feel I could live alone in Algiers."

"I am sure that would be a great mistake."

Kitrina had no intention of telling him that she was not certain whether or not the Villa had belonged to her mother, and that when he arrived she had been searching for something which might have given her the answer to that question.

"I believe when your father was alive," the Sheikh said, "you once visited my *Kasbah*."

"We visited many different tribes," Kitrina replied with a smile, "and I am afraid, *Monsieur,* I do not remember you."

"It was a long time ago," the Sheikh said, "and my father was then the head of the tribe. But I am sure I can remember you as a very pretty little girl."

Kitrina smiled again.

"It is kind of you to say so, although I expect really I was somewhat of a nuisance. I seem to recall people being surprised that a child of my age should be travelling about the desert with my parents and staying in all sorts of strange places."

She thought that sounded slightly rude and added quickly:

"And some very comfortable and attractive ones!"

"That is what my *Kasbah* is," the Sheikh said. "I am Sheikh Hassan El Abdulah. I therefore suggest, *Mademoiselle* that as you have nowhere else to go, you come back with me."

Kitrina stared at him thinking she did not understand what he was saying, and he went on:

"You are very beautiful and you shall be my Chief Wife. I will divorce the woman who has that position now, and you shall take her place."

Kitrina felt he could not be serious until she saw his eyes and felt suddenly afraid.

"It is very . . flattering, *Monsieur,*" she said quickly, "but my answer is 'No'! I have no . . wish to be . . married, and I must . . return to . . Florence."

Because she was frightened she rose to her feet and the Sheikh rose too.

"Now you are being foolish," he said. "I can offer you comfort and security, and you will be very happy with me. All women are happy when I make them mine!"

He spoke with a note of passion in his voice that made

Kitrina want to run away from him, and hide herself.

Then her instinct made her aware that if she lost her dignity he would lose his.

With a composure she was far from feeling, and almost as if her father was beside her telling her what to do, she said:

"I am deeply honoured by what you have . . suggested to me, but you will understand it would be . . impossible for me to make a . . hasty judgement or decide my . . future without considering the full implications of what it would . . mean to be your . . wife."

"You will be my Chief Wife," the Sheikh repeated, "and will rule my household when my mother is dead, and my other wives will obey you and wait upon you."

As Kitrina knew this was what happened in an Arab *Harem* she merely inclined her head and he continued:

"I will not take 'No' for an answer, but now as the *Comte* is not here I must find somebody else to sign the papers which I had brought for him and which refer to the arrangements that he made with me last month."

"I am sure there must be somebody in Algiers who has taken his place," Kitrina said.

She was attempting to speak calmly, although her voice was trembling.

"That I will find out," the Sheikh replied, "although it may take a little time."

Kitrina snatched at the word.

"I need time," she said, "time to think, time to pack up what I need. You will understand, *Monsieur*, that I have only just arrived here."

"Of course I understand," the Sheikh replied. "I will collect you tomorrow."

He looked around the room and there was a look of avarice in his eyes.

"You are right to take what is yours, and not leave it to be stolen or neglected. Get the servants to pack everything for you. I will pay them when I come."

"I . . understand," Kitrina managed to say.

He did not speak, he merely looked at her.

She felt as if he stripped her of everything she wore and a

fear swept through her body as if the fire in his eyes burned her.

He salaamed, but it was the gesture of a Ruler, a man of authority, and it was as if already he owned her and she was his.

There was a smile on his lips as he left.

When he had gone she put her hands up to her eyes and knew that she was trembling all over.

She knew enough about Africa to know that the Sheikh meant exactly what he said and there would be no escape unless when he returned she was not there.

Her first impulse was to send for a carriage and drive immediately to the harbour and board the first ship that would take her away from Algiers.

Then she thought it would be a mistake to leave without any possessions.

Calling the old servants she sent them hurrying for help. She was quite certain they had relations or friends within reach, and at least she had time to take some of her Mother's things with her.

She soon found where the huge round leather trunks that had travelled many miles, sometimes on the backs of camels, sometimes in bullock-carts, were kept.

They were battered and scratched and with two exceptions, very much the worse for wear.

But they would, Kitrina thought, hold a great many of her Mother's possessions she wished to keep.

She made the servants work all the rest of the evening and far into the night, and she rose at dawn to finish packing what was left.

As the sun began to grow hotter she drove down to the dock and found a ship which would carry her away from Africa, and from the Sheikh.

Chapter Four

Kitrina went into the Study to find a book to read.

The Marquis had said that he had an appointment with his Solicitors and he saw no reason for her to accompany him.

"It is hot today," he said, "and I suggest you rest after a hard ride this morning, and we will do something later in the afternoon."

Kitrina gave him a radiant smile, thinking that everything he planned was more thrilling than the last, and she had never thought she would be so happy as she was staying with him.

She had no idea that all the time he was worried as to what he would do with her when he left Paris.

Every morning he told himself he must have a serious talk with her.

And yet each time that he saw her, so excited about what they were to do and so enthusiastic all the time they were together, he found it impossible to take the smile from her face, and to make her consider the stark reality of her future.

He himself also had enjoyed their rides in the Bois, and the times when he took her out to luncheon at different Restaurants to meet his friends.

He had taken the line of least resistance by explaining that Kitrina was his Ward, and had avoided where possible calling her by his name.

Instead it had been easy when his friends were French to say:

"This is my Ward, Kitrina!"

The Frenchmen immediately addressed her as *Mademoiselle* while the women had, the Marquis knew, looked at her enviously.

At the same time, both the men and the women had thought she was still quite young and would have been surprised to learn that she was in fact, eighteen and her birthday had taken place the previous day.

The Marquis had given her as a present a small charm bracelet with little gold souvenirs of Paris on it.

He thought that of all the gifts he had ever given a woman, none could have more genuinely delighted its recipient.

"I have always longed for a charm bracelet," Kitrina had cried, "But never thought I would have one."

The Marquis had deliberately bought something very simple and in comparison to what he had given the Countess of Sandford and Millie, very inexpensive.

He had thought it would be a mistake to let people suspect that Kitrina occupied a somewhat reprehensible position in his life, as they would if she wore diamonds or any other precious stones.

The charm bracelet became her and he thought nothing could look more graceful on her thin wrist as she held it up for him to admire.

"Thank you, thank you!" she said over and over again.

He found himself wondering if in the years to come she would be so enthusiastic about a simple charm bracelet.

It was impossible not to realise that every Frenchman eyed her admiringly.

The Marquis was sure it was only because Kitrina seemed so young that there were not a dozen young men calling at the house, leaving bouquets and invitations.

There were, as it happened, quite a number of his friends who now knew he was in Paris, but he made various excuses for not accepting invitations either to large or to intimate dinners.

Whenever he considered that he might perhaps take Kitrina to a Reception or a *Soirée,* he thought after some consideration that it would be a mistake.

What had really happened was that he had got no further in his search for a solution to her problem from the moment when he had taken her from Celeste's house to his own.

'What am I to do? What the devil am I to do?' he asked himself, not only night after night, but a dozen times each day when they were riding in the Bois or talking about the adventurous life she had lived as a child when her parents were alive.

He had found it even more surprising, when they argued over some abstract literary theory or some fundamental principle, political or international, that was being discussed in the newspapers.

He was aware that Kitrina's mother had been right when she said the Elkes were as a whole a very clever family.

But he had not expected Kitrina to show an intelligence which he had seldom found before in any woman, let alone in one so young.

He had bought her a number of gowns, not only because he thought it was his duty to see that she was properly dressed, but also, although he hesitated to admit it to himself, because he enjoyed creating a frame for her very unusual looks.

Because he had exceedingly good taste, the Marquis had always himself dressed his mistresses, after ensconcing them in discreet little houses in St. John's Wood.

The Social Beauties, because they knew how fastidious he was and wished to please him, invariably asked his opinion when they were buying gowns of any importance.

This was often because they hoped he would pay for them. At the same time, it rather amused him, unlike most Englishmen, to know what suited a woman best.

He often thought women were lamentably foolish when they followed what was the fashion, whether it became them or not.

Everything that Kitrina wore seemed in some way to take on her personality.

The Marquis was very careful not to let her look overdressed or to wear gowns that were too old for her, and he was aware that in white and soft pastel shades she invariably looked even more like a small angel and the gown became part of her personality and character.

'She is unique!' he found himself saying, and wondered

what the Elke family would think of her if they ever met her.

He shied away from the thought of how shocked they would be that she even existed, and the vitriolic things they would say about her father.

Everything that had been said against him in the past would be resurrected and, if she heard it, which was inevitable, Kitrina would in consequence be deeply hurt and distressed.

'How am I to protect her from all that?' he asked.

Once again there was no reply to his question.

She had only been with him for four days, but with Kitrina every moment of them had been for him a sheer delight.

She acquiesced in everything the Marquis wished to do, and strangely enough, for it was very unusual for him, he was quite content just to be with her.

Although he had intended to spend his time in Paris in a very different manner, he never gave his original plans a thought.

He had however felt somehow guilty at not having communicated with Celeste and, though he had told Kitrina he had a business meeting with his Solicitors, he was in fact, going to visit Celeste.

He was intending to tell her what he had accomplished so far – which was nothing.

Celeste was the only person with whom he could discuss Kitrina, and he hoped perhaps she would have some suggestions which he had not yet thought of himself, although what they could be he had no idea.

It was impossible for him to take Kitrina with him so he left her in the house.

He knew that she would be perfectly happy reading either the books which covered the walls of his Study, or else the newspapers and magazines which were automatically ordered for him as soon as he arrived in Paris.

"I shall not be long," he said.

He drove away, looking very distinguished with his tall hat on one side of his dark head, and the silver bridles on his horses which were engraved with his crest glinting in the sunshine.

As he went, Kitrina watching until he was out sight thought a little wistfully that she would have liked to go with him.

She had never imagined before how thrilling it would be to be with a man, to hold his attention, and to talk to him almost as if they were equals.

'He is so kind to me,' she thought, 'and although I must seem to him very ignorant at times, he never makes me feel ignorant or stupid, as I am sure I really am.'

She had not failed to notice that, when they met beautifully dressed and very attractive ladies who held out their gloved hands to the Marquis with delight, their eyes sparkled and there was often what seemed to Kitrina to be an invitation in them.

'He finds them attractive,' she told herself, 'and it is not surprising.'

She wanted to know more about the Marquis, but she was too shy to ask him why he had never married.

She was certain however it was something he would do one day, simply because he would want a son to take over his position when he was dead, and carry on the title.

She could remember her father saying how important a position the Marquis of Elkesley held, and he had described the estate when his father had lived at Elke Castle.

Kitrina had listened, as if to a fairy-story, when she spoke of the army of servants that had been needed to run the huge house, the footmen, all over six feet tall, who were in attendance in the great marble hall.

"They wore the family livery, and the horses had a luxurious stable with never," her father had said laughingly, "a straw out of place."

'Will the Marquis ever take me there?' Kitrina wondered.

She knew it was a house she longed to see because of her father's description of it.

The Marquis had however not talked of returning to England, and for the first time she wondered why he had not told her more about her Elke relations.

Instead of going to the bookshelf to choose a book to read, she stood in front of a gilt-framed mirror which was hanging above the carved gilt table which matched it, and looked at herself.

'He will be proud of me in my new gowns,' she told her reflection.

She thought the way her hair was arranged very simply at the back of her head was also attractive.

Yet because she was very sensitive and very perceptive, she was aware, now she thought of it, that there was some barrier between herself and the Marquis.

She had been conscious of it yesterday, or perhaps the day before, and she knew this was definitely something she must face and she would have to ask him what was wrong.

She was not certain if 'wrong' was the right word, and yet the feeling was there that he was not being entirely frank with her.

However why she should think that and be so certain of it, she could not explain.

'I will talk to him when he comes back,' she thought.

Then she felt a shiver of fear in case he should be angry because she was inquisitive.

Although he was so kind to her, she knew — perhaps it was because he was so much older – that he was a rather frightening person, even though she thought of him as being very like her father.

She was aware that the servants hurried to do his bidding, and occasionally when he scowled or looked angry she felt apprehensive in case he was cross with her.

'What can it be? What is he keeping from me?' she wondered.

She told herself that could not be the explanation.

Then she was terribly afraid that perhaps the Marquis was finding her, as she had suggested he might, an encumbrance.

He had never said anything to make her feel that, and indeed had seemed to enjoy everything they had done together.

Last night he had taken her to the Opera, and she felt as if he had opened the doors of Fairyland.

In Florence the Schoolgirls had been taken to Concerts, but there was no Opera House. Indeed if there had been, they would not have been allowed to attend it.

The Opera House in Paris, with its gilded walls, its fantastic statues, and an audience which seemed to be part of the fairy-story, was a new experience.

The Marquis had of course taken a box, and Kitrina looking around at the women glittering with jewels in the other boxes found it hard to believe they were not on the stage and part of the Opera itself.

Because she loved music she had been swept away into a magical world where she had forgotten everything but the story unfolding in song until it became more real than reality.

She was not aware that the Marquis was watching her rather than the stage with a little smile on his lips.

When in the traditional manner the heroine wept over her lost lover, Kitrina wept too.

As the curtain fell she found it hard to return to normality and be herself again.

As if he understood what she was feeling, the Marquis had said:

"I think we both deserve some supper after that emotional experience. I will take you somewhere quiet where you can tell me what you felt and what you thought about your first Opera."

It had been difficult to put her feelings into words, but Kitrina had tried.

She remembered how the Marquis had understood, and she was sure no other man would have been so interested in what she felt.

'I am so lucky!' she said to her reflection in the mirror. 'I suppose it is because he is a relation that we think alike and our thoughts do not always have to be translated into words because we sense them.'

Then she told herself that she was wasting time when she might be finding something interesting to talk about to the Marquis when he returned.

She left the mirror to walk across the room to the bookcase.

She was just drawing from a shelf a book which she knew had been written by one of the French authors about whom she had read in the newspapers, when the door of the Study opened.

She looked round eagerly, thinking that perhaps the Marquis had returned sooner than she expected and was suddenly frozen to the spot as the Major Domo announced:

"Sheikh Hassam El Abdullah, *M'mselle,* to see you!"

It had never entered Kitrina's head that she might see the Sheikh in Paris.

In fact, in the last few days she had been so happy with the Marquis that she had ceased to think about him.

Now it was a shock to see him come into the room looking, she thought, dark and sinister in his Arab head-dress and his *djellaba* worn over ordinary clothes which might have been worn by any Frenchman.

She stood holding the novel she had chosen tightly in her hands across her breast as if it was a protection.

As the door closed behind him the Sheikh walked slowly towards her until they were facing each other.

He did not speak as his black eyes seemed to devour her in the same way that they had done in the Villa, and after a moment she said in a very small voice that trembled:

"Why . . are you here? H.how . . did you . . find me?"

"I saw you last night at the Opera," the Sheikh replied, "and I find it extraordinary that you should have run away from Algiers· when I told you I would collect you the following day."

He spoke in French and Kitrina replied in the same language.

"I . . I asked for time to . . think about your proposition, *Monsieur,* and as I could not . . agree to what you . . suggested . . I came to Paris."

"I am not in the habit of being refused by a woman."

Kitrina looked away from him and managed to say, although her lips trembled:

"I . . I am deeply honoured that you should . . ask me to

be your . . wife . . but I am now with the . . head of my father's family . . who will look after me and . . protect me."

"I have learnt that the gentleman who accompanied you last night was the Marquis of Elkesley," the Sheikh said, "but your place, *Mademoiselle,* is in Africa, where your father lived for so many years, and also your mother."

She did not look at him and he said in a rather different tone, with a beguiling note in his voice:

"Come back with me. I promise that you shall have every comfort you require in my *Kasbah,* and you will be of more importance as my Chief Wife than you will ever be here in Paris."

"I . . I do not want to be of . . importance," Kitrina managed to reply. "I want to be . . happy, and I am very happy with my father's . . cousin . . which is where I belong."

"Why should *you* belong," the Sheikh asked, "when your father's family would have nothing to do with him?"

Kitrina gave him a quick glance of surprise and the Sheikh continued:

"I have been told that your father, having run away with your mother, was exiled from England. That was why they lived in Africa until he died. Then after she had been left alone, your mother went to Dakar with the *Comte* de Villeneuve and you were sent to Florence."

"Yes, I know that," Kitrina said, "but I am English, *Monsieur* and I am looking forward to living in England."

"Do you think England will make you happy?" the Sheikh asked. "They were not kind to your father, so why should they be kind to you?"

"My father was very happy in Africa," Kitrina said firmly, "but as I have the choice, I would rather go to England and, although I have never see it, I am sure it is where I belong."

"How can you be certain of that?" the Sheikh asked. "Supposing when you get there you are ostracised as your father was? I have talked to members of my tribe who are old and remember the time when you stayed at my *Kasbah* as a child. They tell me that your father behaved very badly and ran away with the wife of a great Lord. Everybody was angry! You are your father's child! Do you believe they will not be angry with you?"

The way he spoke made Kitrina feel apprehensive in a way she had not felt before.

Because she knew why he was saying such things, she feared he was fighting a battle which he must win.

"I am very honoured . . *Monsieur*," she said, "that you should be . . interested in my . . welfare, but I must make the . . decision about my own life, and I have . . decided that I wish to go to . . England."

"And I have decided," the Sheikh said. "that you shall come back to Africa with me!"

He took a step towards her as he spoke and Kitrina backed away from him until she was standing with her shoulders against the bookcase.

"You are very beautiful!" he said in a low voice. "I want you! I want you, and I intend to have you!"

"You have no . . right to say . . such things to . . me," Kitrina retorted. "Please . . go away and . . leave me . . alone!"

"That is something I have no intention of doing," the Sheikh replied. "When I leave, I shall take you with me, and you will live in the desert as you did with your father, and will find it very enjoyable."

He took another step nearer to her and Kitrina gave a little scream as she said:

"Do not . . touch me! Go away . . you have no . . right to come here . . and threaten . . me!"

"I am not threatening you," the Sheikh said. "I am only telling you that you are mine, and as my wife you will be far more content than you will ever be in England, where your father's relations will really have no use for you."

"That is not true!" Kitrina cried. "I am here with the Marquis, who is my . . Guardian! He . . wants me . . of course he does . . and I shall go . . back to England with him!"

"You will come back to Africa with me!" the Sheikh insisted.

Now the expression in his eyes and the threat of his words was so frightening that Kitrina cringed away from him.

But she was restricted by the bookcase behind her, and knew that if she tried to evade him he would merely catch hold of her.

"Go away!" she cried again. "Go away and . . leave me . . alone! I will never marry you . . never . . never!"

Her voice seemed to ring out and now there was an unpleasant smile on the Sheikh's lips which was more terrifying than if he had actually said anything.

He put out his arms to try to take hold of her, and as Kitrina gave another scream the door opened.

For a moment she could hardly believe that she was saved, and it was the Marquis who stood there.

As the Sheikh turned his head, then dropped his arms, she ran past him and flung herself against the Marquis, dropping the book as she did so to cling to the lapels of his coat with both her hands.

He did not put his arms around her, but merely stared over her head at the Sheikh standing on the other side of the room.

"What is all this about?" he demanded.

His voice was like the crack of a whip, but the Sheikh was not intimidated by it.

He merely drew himself up and faced the Marquis in a manner which proclaimed all too clearly that he considered himself to be on equal terms.

"I called, My Lord," he said, "in order to renew a proposition I have already made to *Mademoiselle* Kitrina."

"A proposition?"

"I asked *Mademoiselle* when she was in Africa to be my Chief Wife," the Sheikh answered, "a proposition of importance which, as she has lived so long in my country, she is capable of appreciating."

"And what was *Mademoiselle's* reply?" the Marquis asked coldly.

The Sheikh's thick lips twisted in a smile as he said:

"Like most young girls, she is at the moment afraid of marriage, but that is something which does not last long."

"What you are saying is that *Mademoiselle* has refused you," the Marquis said, "in which case there is nothing to discuss."

The Sheikh hesitated a moment. Then he said:

"I think, *Monsieur,* you do not understand what I am offering the daughter of your relative who was exiled from his own country."

"I understand perfectly," the Marquis said, "and as you have received your answer, *Monsieur,* I can only bid you good-day.

The Sheikh's eyes flashed and for a moment the Marquis thought he might threaten him with violence.

The Arab's right hand moved as if instinctively towards the knife he would have carried in his belt if he had not been wearing Western dress.

Then as he met the Marquis's eyes and the two men grappled with each other without words the Sheikh said:

"I will leave your house as you request, *Monsieur,* but I think *Mademoiselle* will regret in the future that she has refused an offer of marriage, an offer which I suspect she has not received from Your Lordship!"

It was a subtle insult made with a bitterness and note of venom in the Sheikh's voice that was unconcealed.

The Marquis however did not reply, but merely indicated without moving as Kitrina still clung to him, the half-open door behind him.

Slowly and with an undeniable dignity which came from years of leadership the Sheikh moved across the room.

Only as he reached the Marquis he glanced for a moment at Kitrina who was still hiding her face, her pale hair vivid against the darkness of the Marquis's coat.

The Sheikh's eyes lingered on her. Then he raised them, blazing with anger, to the Marquis.

Again the two men looked at each other, and the Marquis knew that if they had been in the desert instead of in Paris, the Arab would have killed him.

As it was, holding his head high, the Sheikh passed on and out of the room.

Only when he had gone did the Marquis put one arm around Kitrina and say:

"It is all right, he cannot hurt you."

All the time he had been speaking to the Sheikh he had felt her trembling against him, and he knew how terrified she was.

Now, as if she could hardly believe what he had said was true, she raised her head as if to be quite certain the Sheikh was no longer there.

Then she hid her face once again against the Marquis saying:

"He . . he is dangerous! I know he is . . dangerous!"

"What can he do to hurt you?" the Marquis asked. "He should not have been admitted in the first place. Another time when I leave you I will make certain the servants understand that you are not to receive visitors until I return."

He thought as he spoke how fortunate it was that when he had reached Celeste's house it was to find that she had gone out and he could therefore not see her.

It had then suddenly struck him that he would rather be with Kitrina than do anything else.

He might, he thought now, even have had a presentiment that she needed him and was in trouble.

When he turned his horses round and drove back to his *grande maison* he thought that as it was such a fine afternoon he would take her driving in the Bois.

The servants had told him as soon as he arrived back who was with Kitrina, and as he reached the door of his Study he had heard her scream.

He was, in fact, extremely angry that she should have been frightened in such a manner, and it was something he had not foreseen.

Now he was concerned only with making light of the situation and preventing her from being so frightened.

"Come and sit down," he said, "and I will get you something to drink."

"I . . I do not . . want anything," Kitrina said. "I . . I just want to be . . certain that you are . . here . . and he will not . . take me away . . as he has . . threatened to do."

"I promise you he will not do that," the Marquis answered. "I expect because he believed himself to be of such importance in his own world, he cannot understand why you are not over-joyed at being the Chief of his four wives!"

He tried as he spoke to make it sound amusing, but Kitrina only made a little sound that was not far from tears as she replied:

"He said . . that your family would not . . want me in England . . and my . . rightful place was in Africa."

"Forget him! Forget everything he said!" the Marquis said sharply.

At the same time, he thought the Arab had in fact spoken the truth, and in consequence had made his own task more difficult than it was already.

He drew Kitrina to the sofa, sat her down, and walked to the grog-tray in the corner of the Study.

There was a small jug of freshly-made lemonade and he poured some into a glass for her.

"Drink this," he said, "and then, if you feel strong enough, I had returned to ask you to come driving with me in the Bois."

"You . . you came back . . for me?" Kitrina asked.

There was a different note in her voice now but as she looked up at the Marquis he could still see the tears in her eyes.

"It is such a lovely day," he said, "and I think it would be a pity to waste it."

"Of course," Kitrina agreed. "Shall I go and put on my bonnet?"

"Alternatively we could stay here," the Marquis suggested.

She gave a quick glance around the room almost as if she was afraid the Sheikh might still be there, hiding in the shadows.

"No, no! I would much rather go . . . out with you!"

"Very well," he answered, "but hurry or the horses will become restless."

Kitrina put down the lemonade of which she had taken only a sip.

Then with a smile which he knew was an effort she went from his side, and he heard her footsteps running down the passage.

"Damn the man!" the Marquis swore beneath his breath. "Why did he have to come here upsetting the child?"

The Sheikh apparently had told Kitrina that she would not be welcome in England.

It was the truth – the truth he had not yet been brave enough to tell her. He knew it was something it was impossible for him to say, unless he could find an alternative place for her to live.

It would certainly not be in Africa, nor with the Sheikh, whose way of life and treatment of women was so alien from anything that was English.

He remembered what Celeste had said about him and thought that if she had known of the Sheikh's arrival in Paris, she would have warned him.

'I will somehow see her tomorrow,' the Marquis thought, 'but I will make quite certain that while I am away from the house Kitrina is safe.'

At the same time, he knew it would be impossible for him to be always on hand to protect her, and once again he wondered frantically what he could do about her and where she could go.

* * *

Driving in the Bois Kitrina felt the terror that had gripped her like a physical pain begin to subside.

The Sheikh had gone, she was sitting beside the Marquis, and she told herself there was nothing now for her to worry about.

However she could not help remembering what he had said, and when they were driving a little more slowly under the shady trees she said:

"You have not told me very much about Papa's relations

in England. Will they really be . . angry with me because . .
so long ago . . they were . . angry with Papa?"

The Marquis concentrated on his horses and there was a
definite pause before he replied:

"Your father, in running away with your mother, upset a
great many people."

"I am sure, although I never discussed it with Papa, that
he was sorry to do that, but he always said that love was
more important than anything else, and he loved Mama so
very, very much!"

The Marquis could not think of anything to say, so he
remained silent.

After they had driven for a little while Kitrina said:

"I . . I never thought of it until now . . but perhaps your
family would not be pleased to . . see me . . and would not
be . . kind to me as . . you have been."

This, the Marquis thought, was his opportunity to
explain the very difficult position she was in.

At that moment however there was a carriage coming
towards them so swiftly that it was imperative for him to
pull his horses to the side of the road, and he could not both
drive and talk.

Only when the danger was past did Kitrina give a little
sigh and say:

"You drive so beautifully, just as you ride. Papa used to
say that all the Elkes had a way with horses that was
something they had inherited when they were born."

"I think that is true," the Marquis agreed, "and I suppose I like riding and driving more than anything else."

"Especially when you have such magnificent horses!"
Kitrina said. "They must miss you when you are away from
Paris for a long time, and I expect your horses in England
are longing for you to go back."

It seemed for the moment as if Kitrina had forgotten her
question about the attitude of her father's relations.

Although it seemed the wrong place to talk seriously on
such a difficult problem, the Marquis now cursed himself
silently for being such a coward as he talked instead about
horses.

He promised without really thinking about it to take Kitrina racing and she was so excited at the prospect that they arrived back at the house before anything more could be said about meeting her relatives.

Only when she had gone upstairs to change for dinner did the Marquis ask himself when he was going to stop being so feeble and behave like a man about the problem of Kitrina.

'I must see Celeste first,' he repeated to himself.

Then he knew that once again he was evading the issue.

*　　*　　*

Upstairs, lying in a scented bath which had been prepared for her by a lady's maid, Kitrina was worrying over what the Sheikh had said.

She was no longer frightened that he could abduct her, for the Marquis was there to protect her from him.

At the same time, she could not erase from her mind his warning that she would be unwelcome in England and the only possible place in which she could feel at home was Africa.

'Papa could not go back,' she reasoned, 'but surely that does not apply to me?'

She remembered the Marquis had not answered her question and she told herself she would ask him again.

She hoped that when he did take her back, as she felt sure he intended to do, his relatives would not criticise him.

'He has been so kind to me, and he has given me all these beautiful clothes and my charm bracelet,' Kitrina thought. 'I could not bear to think of his being criticised for taking me to England.'

Then a streak of fear shot through her as she realised that if she did not go to England, or he did not take her, there would be nowhere else for her to go.

Once again the Sheikh was menacing her, and she felt as if she could see his black eyes looking at her and hypnotising her into doing what he wanted.

Then she told herself she was being very fanciful.

The Marquis had sent him away, which he would

consider as an insult. But because there was nothing he could do about it, he would probably dismiss it and pretend it had never happened.

Then she recalled that an insult to somebody of the Sheikh's importance could only be revenged in blood.

'I will not think about it! It cannot happen here in Paris!' Kitrina told herself desperately.

And yet she was remembering the stories she had heard in the past of terrible acts of vengeance taken by one tribe upon another.

There had been pitched battles, deliberate murders, and men left wounded to die miserably and have their flesh eaten from their bones by vultures.

Everything she had learnt about tribal warfare but which had lain dormant at the back of her mind now came back to haunt her like ghosts from the past.

'How can I be so stupid as to think that the Sheikh could do anything dangerous in a civilised City like Paris?' she asked.

At the same time, as she dressed herself in one of her new gowns before going downstairs to dine with the Marquis, she knew she was afraid.

Not only for herself, but for him.

Chapter Five

"There is only one thing you can do, *Mon Cher*," Celeste said, "and you should have thought of it yourself."

"I imagined I had thought of everything possible!" the Marquis said dryly.

He was sitting in Celeste's bedroom, and as usual she was looking very alluring against her silk and lace pillows.

This morning she was wearing a bed-jacket which was a froth of lace trimmed with green ribbons which seemed to echo the green in her eyes.

There was also a faint smile on her attractive lips as she realised how worried the Marquis was.

When he told her that the Sheikh had come to his house yesterday and terrified Kitrina, Celeste had exclaimed angrily:

"*C'est intolérable!* How dare he do such a thing? If I had known he was in Paris, I would have warned you."

"I thought you would have done that," the Marquis replied, "but he made me realise that things cannot go on as they are, and anyway I will have to return to England sometime."

"Of course," Celeste agreed, "and my solution is quite easy. You must take Kitrina with you and become her protector!"

The Marquis was so astonished that he sat upright in his chair and stared at Celeste as if he could not have heard her aright.

"Are you really suggesting . . .?" he began.

"But of course!" Celeste interrupted, "You say you cannot marry her, and that I understand. Like a Frenchman you have to marry somebody of the same importance as yourself. At the same time you cannot abandon this poor child, and the Sheikh will not leave her alone as long as she is in Paris."

The Marquis did not speak and Celeste added with a little smile:

"Anyway she would not be alone for long, and you know as well as I do no Frenchman would offer her marriage."

"I never thought . . ." the Marquis began.

Then as his voice faded away he knew that Kitrina was very attractive, so attractive that she had occupied his thoughts every moment since they had been together, and he had lain awake at night thinking about her.

"What is important to any young girl," Celeste was saying in a soft voice, "is to be initiated into the joy of love by a man who is kind, gentle and understanding, as I was by André de Villeneuve."

She looked at the Marquis and there was a different note in her voice as she said:

"You are all those things, *Mon Brave*. and you are also the Dream Lover whom all women want to find. I would be very surprised if Kitrina was not in love with you already!"

The Marquis rose from the chair and as if he could not sit still, walked about the bedroom.

"I imagined she thought of me as a second father," he said lamely.

Celeste laughed.

"You are far too young to be her father, and no woman could think of you except as a very attractive, very masculine man."

The Marquis still paced up and down and she said;

"You must see there is really nothing else you can do! Kitrina will be very happy with you in England, I am certain of that, and you can change her name, so that none of your relatives will have any idea who she really is."

The Marquis went to the window and stood looking out with unseeing eyes, into the sunlit street.

Celeste watched him with a tender expression on her lovely face of which he was not aware.

She had not forgotten how happy she had been when the Marquis had spent all the time he was in Paris with her, and the fires within them had leapt so fiercely that they were both consumed by them.

But like all fires they had eventually died down, though Celeste knew that the Marquis had a special place in her heart which would never be filled by anybody else.

He turned from the window to say:

"I shall certainly think over what you have suggested. Thank you, Celeste for being so sympathetic."

"I would not like to think of little Kitrina in any hands but yours," she said. "If she is to wake up and face the world as it really is, at least the awakening will be gentle and not the violent and terrifying shock it would be with most other men."

As she spoke they were both thinking of the Sheikh, and the Marquis's lips tightened while there was a hard look in his eyes.

Then without saying any more, he kissed Celeste goodbye and went outside to where his Chaise was waiting.

He had left Kitrina alone at his house, but he had given instructions that she was to sleep late, and when she awoke her breakfast was to be taken to her in bed.

If there were any callers, she was not to be told of them, and one of the maids was to be in attendance upon her until his return.

Like Kitrina, he was well aware that he had insulted the Sheikh and that the consequences would be serious. He was thinking as he drove back that the sooner they left Paris the better.

At the same time it had never entered his head that he should make Kitrina his mistress.

He knew it must be wrong, simply because she looked so young and so exactly like a small angel that even to think of her being made love to was a kind of sacrilege.

Yet in the new gowns he had bought for her she was very much a woman, and he knew if he was honest that nothing could be more attractive or more fascinating than to awaken anyone so beautiful, pure and untouched, to the ecstasy of love.

He knew Celeste had been right in saying Kitrina's first lover should be kind, gentle and understanding, and he hoped he would be all those things.

Thinking of her, he realised she was like a white rosebud, or perhaps a better simile would be an unopened lily not yet touched by the rays of the sun.

He was aware that the rapt expression in her eyes and in her voice when she greeted him in the morning, or when he returned to her from having been away, was not entirely that of a daughter to a father.

Although she might not realise it, he was already in her eyes a man, and he remembered how yesterday she had turned to him in fear and her whole body had trembled against his.

Because he was anxious about her he drove a little faster, and although he told himself it was ridiculous he felt a touch of fear as he arrived back at his house just in case anything had happened to her while he had been away.

As he entered the hall there was a cry of joy that was like the sound of a lark rising in the sky as Kitrina came running down the stairs.

"I was waiting for you!" she said. "I was afraid you had forgotten about me."

"How could I possibly do that?" the Marquis asked in a deep voice.

She was looking unusually lovely, he thought, in a white gown trimmed with *broderie anglaise*, the insertions above it slotted through with satin ribbons, the colour of her eyes.

She carried in her hand the little hat he had bought her at the same time as the dress, which had a small brim trimmed with cornflowers and marguerite daises.

When she put it on for his inspection it had made her look very young, and it also made him think of Persephone returning from the darkness of Hades to bring back Spring to the world.

Now her pale gold hair gleamed in the sunshine coming through the windows in the hall, and as she reached him the Marquis thought she was enveloped in a light which could only have come from within herself.

"Did you finish your business?" she asked a little breathlessly.

He remembered he had told her he was going, not to see Celeste, but to complete the business with his Solicitors which he had been unable to finalise yesterday.

"I thought you would like a drive in the Bois this morning," he replied, "and we can ride later in the afternoon when it is cooler."

"I would adore that," Kitrina said, "and can we go our special way?"

"Yes, of course!" the Marquis laughed.

What Kitrina called 'their special way' was a part of the Bois that was not fashionable and where there was therefore very little traffic.

Kitrina had been thrilled with trees which almost met across the roadway, their green leaves giving protection from the sun, and also making mysterious patterns that had caught her fancy.

The Marquis had never before driven in the Bois with a woman who had no wish to show herself off being in his company and aware that she was the envy of her friends because of the smartness of his Chaise and his horses.

It was a new experience to have Kitrina choose the more isolated part of the Bois, and now he wondered if it was not only because she found it beautiful, but also because she would have there no rivals for his attention.

"What does she feel about me?" he asked himself.

He found it impossible not to think all the time about Celeste's suggestion of what he should do with her.

Kitrina had put on her hat in front of one of the mirrors in the hall and it made her, the Marquis thought, look younger than usual.

Her eyes seemed to dance in the sunshine, and her lips curled excitedly.

'Lips,' the Marquis thought, 'that have never been kissed.'

They drove off and at first he had to concentrate on manoeuvring his horses through a considerable amount of traffic in the Champs Élysées.

Then they reached the Bois and turned away on a side road in the direction which Kitrina called 'their special way'.

There was a groom in a small seat behind them, who could not hear what they were saying, and the Marquis asked in his deep voice:

"Are you happy?"

"So happy," Kitrina answered softly, "that I feel as if I could dance on the lake or fly high in the sky."

"I should be very worried if you did that," the Marquis said, "for then I might lose you."

There was a little silence, until Kitrina asked:

"Perhaps you would be . . glad to be . . rid of me!"

"I think you are fishing for compliments," the Marquis answered, "but actually I could not lose you now, Kitrina!"

The way he spoke made her look up as if she thought she had not heard him correctly.

Then she said:

"It is so wonderful . . so very, very wonderful . . being with you! At the same time, I know it cannot last for . . ever."

The Marquis was thinking of how he should reply when ahead of them they saw a small crowd gathered in the centre of the road.

He began to pull in his horses and Kitrina asked:

"Has there been an accident?"

"I do not know," the Marquis replied.

The people ahead were in one of the leafy tunnels which Kitrina liked so much.

The way was narrow and as they made no effort to move the Marquis was obliged to rein in his horses and bring them to a standstill.

As he did so a young man poorly dressed came running towards him saying:

"*Monsieur, Monsieur!* Please come and help!"

"What is the matter?" the Marquis enquired.

"A boy has been injured! I think he is dying! *Vite! Vite!* We need you!"

It flashed through the Marquis's mind that he should send his groom.

Then he remembered that he had come to Paris from England with his horses and could not speak French.

Accordingly he said over his shoulder:

"Take the reins, Jim."

He stepped down from the Chaise.

He had stopped his horses a little distance from the crowd who had their backs to him, concealing whatever was the cause of their concern.

As he walked away from the Chaise, looking very dignified and extremely distinguished, Kitrina watched him, wondering what could possibly have happened.

She suspected that it might be a young boy playing under the trees who had suddenly rushed out into the road and been knocked down by a passing carriage.

She was pondering over it when a voice behind her said:

"If you please, *M'mselle*, Milor' asks you to join him."

She thought as she listened that the voice was not unlike that of the one who had come begging for the Marquis's help.

Instinctively she looked to see where he was and realised that he was now surrounded by the crowd and she could only just see the top of his hat.

"*Monsieur* says come at once, *M'mselle!*" the boy insisted, speaking in a *patois* that was difficult to understand.

"Yes . . of course," Kitrina agreed.

He put out one dirty hand to assist her to the ground, but she managed without him and would have turned to hurry towards the Marquis, when suddenly from behind her, hidden by the Chaise, this man seized her arms.

At the same time a heavy hand came down over her mouth and she was dragged backwards.

It was impossible for her even to scream.

Somebody picked up her feet and she thought it was the boy who had spoken to her.

Then so swiftly that she could hardly realise what was happening, she was carried away into the trees at the side of the road.

The heavy hand was still over her mouth, and she could only wonder where the men were taking her, and knew it was impossible for her even to struggle against them.

Then with a stab of terror that seemed to strike through her like a knife, she knew who was responsible for her abduction and where she was going.

A few minutes later, gagged and bound, she was being driven away in a closed carriage with the blinds down over the windows so that she could not even see her captors.

She was sure there were three of them inside the carriage with her, and she thought that a fourth had joined the coachman on the box.

The carriage was travelling at a tremendous pace, and as Kitrina was half-lying, half-sitting on the seat with her legs straight out in front of her, her ankles roped together, she was exceedingly uncomfortable.

There was also a rope round her waist that tied her hands down to her sides, and a handkerchief gagged her mouth, although she realised that even if it was not there, it would be quite useless for her to scream.

The men in the carriage did not speak but she could hear them breathing and she was sure if she could see them their dark skins would tell her they were Arabs.

It was unnecessary to ask who had sent them to take her prisoner.

The Marquis had saved her before, but how would he realise what had happened to her now?

If he suspected she was being taken to the Sheikh and followed her, it might be too late.

Too late to prevent the Sheikh from making her his wife as he wanted her to be.

Her whole being cried out at the horror of it, and she told herself that she must die before that happened, but how she could do so, she had no idea.

The carriage was still moving very swiftly, but Kitrina knew they were in traffic and occasionally the horses were pulled up sharply as if to avoid a collision.

They would start off again with a jerk and she knew the coachman was using his whip.

Then there was the sound of a gate or a door being opened and a minute or so later the horses came to a standstill.

She thought now that she would be taken to the Sheikh and in her terror she began to pray:

'Help me . . God, let the . . Marquis save me . . please . . God . . please!'

Even as she prayed she knew it was hopeless.

She thought her father and her mother had forgotten her and she was alone and helpless.

Then somebody opened the door of the carriage, the light streamed in and she could see they were outside the open door of what appeared to be a stable.

Two of the men lifted her out and she was carried inside.

She knew she had been right in thinking it was a stable when she smelt hay and the scent of horses.

It was very dark, and she could not think why they were carrying her into what must be a stall.

Then suddenly the men, supporting her one at her feet and one under her shoulders, lowered her and she found herself in a narrow box.

Then as she lay in it, thinking how restricting it was, though it seemed to fit her, she was aware with a feeling of abject horror which was more agonizing then anything she had known before, that she was in a coffin.

The men pressed in the folds of her skirt, and then as with a frantic effort to save herself, Kitrina tried to sit up, they pushed her shoulders down again.

The next minute the lid of the coffin covered her and she could hear it being screwed down.

'I shall suffocate slowly,' she thought in horror and knew it was a death far worse than if she had been stabbed in the heart and died quickly.

Then the coffin was lifted up off the ground and carried out of the stable.

It was then she was aware that just below the lid on either side of the coffin there were little specks of light and she knew they were air-holes to prevent her from suffocating.

Just for a minute it was some consolation.

Then the terror enveloped her again because she knew it would be impossible now for the Marquis to find her, for who would suspect that the Sheikh was taking her away as a corpse?

'What . . can I do? Oh . . God . . what can . . I do?' Kitrina prayed.

But there was no answer, only once again the rumble of wheels.

*   *   *

It must have been over an hour later before Kitrina was aware that the men were undoing the screws which had held down the lid of the coffin.

As they did so there was no hope in her heart that she might be rescued, for she was aware that she had been taken in the coffin to a Railway Station, and carried a long way down a platform before being placed in a train.

There was a great deal of talk between what she supposed were French Railway Officials and her captors.

Finally she was dumped down on the floor of what she thought must be a luggage van and again there was considerable chatter which told her that forms were being signed by her captors.

She was by now so stiff and cramped that she felt as if every bone in her body ached and there was also so little air coming through the holes in the sides of the coffin that she found it hard to breathe.

Finally the train started and once again there was the rumble of wheels under her, only this time they were on a railway-track.

Suddenly the lid was raised and seeing a number of dark faces peering down at her she knew, as she had suspected, they were Arabs.

Because she could speak Arabic she understood when one of them said:

"It's all right. She's alive."

"Much trouble for us if she'd died!" another man remarked.

"You're right," a third replied. "Let's release her. He said we could."

They untied the rope around Kitrina's legs and the one which encircled her waist, while another man removed the handkerchief which had gagged her mouth.

At first she found it impossible to move her arms or even her hands.

Then as the blood began to flow back into her limbs it was painful.

The Arabs lifted her out of the coffin and onto a chair and she saw what she had not expected, that she was in a private Car which very rich men either possessed or could hire privately and have attached to the end of a train.

Feeling helplessly limp after being tied up for so long and from lack of air, and also numb with fear, she just sat in the chair as the train gathered speed, looking at the Arabs who were staring at her.

Then one of them fetched her a glass of water, and she found she was so weak that she had to hold it very tightly with both hands before she could drink.

"You are all right, *Mademoiselle?*" one of the men asked in very bad French.

"I am . . alive!" Kitrina answered in Arabic. "But you have kidnapped me, and that in France is a crime for which if you are . . caught you will be severely . . punished and perhaps sentenced to death by the guillotine!"

She meant to speak not only bravely but aggressively, but instead even to herself her voice sounded weak and rather feeble.

She knew the men were impressed that she could speak their language, and one of them sitting down opposite her, who she thought was in charge of the others, said:

"We're only obeying orders, *Mademoiselle*, and we've been careful not to hurt you. You can have anything you wish while we are journeying to Marseilles."

"Marseilles!"

Kitrina held her breath and could hardly breathe the word.

Knowing now where they were going, she knew for certain who would be waiting for her either at Marseilles, or when they reached the coast of Africa.

She shut her eyes with the horror of it and one of the Arabs said in a whisper:

"If she dies, he'll have our heads off our bodies!"

"She needs rest," the man in charge said firmly. "Carry her to the bed."

Kitrina would have protested, but he took the glass from her hands and two the men picked her up and carried her to the bedroom which opened out from the Drawing-Room Car.

They laid her down gently on the bed, and she knew from the expressions on their faces they were worried in case anything should happen to her, for which they would incur the wrath of the Sheikh.

Because at least she could use her authority with them she said:

"Leave me. I will . . sleep!"

They hesitated and she knew they were wondering if there was any means by which she could escape, but finally on the order of their leader they went back into the Drawing-Room Car leaving the door of her compartment ajar.

She knew that actually there was nothing she could do, for even if she tried to fling herself from the train when it was moving she would have first to open a door or a window, which they would be able to prevent her from doing.

She would have to endure their hands upon her and be much more uncomfortable than if she lay on the bed. There she could at least pray, knowing that however impassioned her prayers might be, there could be no answer to them.

Nevertheless she found herself praying not to God, not

to her father and mother, but to the Marquis.

'Come . . to me . . save me,' she called in her heart.

She could see his handsome face, his eyes looking down into hers, and feel again the magnetism of him which she had felt when she was sitting close to him just before he had been tricked into leaving her.

Then as she remembered how he had said he could not lose her, she knew despairingly she had lost him.

"I shall . . never see . . you again," she whispered, "but . . I love you!"

*   *   *

The Marquis on reaching the crowd that had blocked his way on the road saw a young boy lying on the ground.

His eyes were closed and his dirty face appeared to be streaked with blood.

"What happened?" the Marquis asked of the youths who were pressing round him.

He had reached the boy's body, and as they encircled him from behind he said sharply:

"Stand back! If he is injured he needs air!"

They did not obey him however, even though he spoke in the authoritative tone which normally ensured that his orders were put into operation immediately.

Instead they all started to talk at once, telling him a garbled tale of how the boy had been knocked down by a large brake drawn by four horses which had galloped on and had not stopped to attend to him.

"First," the Marquis said, "we must get him off the road. Then we can see if there are any bones broken."

He looked again at the boy's face and it flashed through his mind that the red marks on it looked more like paint than blood.

Then as he told himself he must be mistaken, one of the crowd still pressing round him gave a whistle.

Quite suddenly, to the Marquis's astonishment, the boy on the ground jumped to his feet and started to run towards the trees.

The other youths followed him so quickly that almost before he could realise what was happening, the Marquis

95

found he was standing alone in an empty road, except for his Chaise that was some distance away.

"I suppose it was just a joke," he told himself angrily, and thought it was not at all amusing.

He walked quickly back to his Chaise and only when he reached it did he realise that Jim holding the reins, was alone, and there was a frightened expression on his face.

"Where is Miss Kitrina?" the Marquis asked sharply.

"Oi dunno, M'Lord," Jim replied. "Some boy spoke to 'er in French, an' she gets down out of th' Chaise, and seemed to go be'ind it. By the time Oi looks round, Oi sees some men carryin' her off through th' trees."

"You saw what?" the Marquis asked, his voice ringing out.

" 'Er bein' carried away, M'Lord, but Oi didn't know wot t'do about it."

For a moment the Marquis felt like cursing the groom, who he had always known was stupid, and telling him he should have shouted to him.

Then as he knew what had happened to Kitrina he merely said sharply: "Give me the reins!" and climbed into the Chaise.

He took off at break-neck speed not to his house as he had first intended, but to Celeste's.

He was wondering frantically all the time he drove towards the Rue du Faubourg St. Honoré what he would do if she was not there.

To his relief as he arrived she was coming out of her front-door escorted by a Frenchman who was well-known to him and whom he had met on various occasions.

The Marquis drew in his horses, handed the reins to Jim and jumped down to the ground.

One look at his face told Celeste before he spoke that something unpleasant had happened.

"What is it?" she asked.

"The Sheikh has kidnapped Kitrina!" the Marquis said abruptly. "Where does he stay when he is in Paris?"

"Kidnapped?" Celeste exclaimed.

"Where does he stay?" the Marquis asked again.

He waited impatiently until Celeste answered:

"I think, in fact I am sure, he stays at the *Continental*."

She looked at her escort as she spoke and said:

"We are speaking, Jacques, of Sheikh Hassam El Abdullah. I remember you said you disliked him. Am I not right in thinking that he stays at the *Continental* when he is in Paris?"

"Now you mention it," the Frenchman replied. "I saw him going in there yesterday afternoon, and hoped I should not be forced to meet him while he is here."

"Thank you," the Marquis said.

Without another word he went back to his Chaise to take the reins from Jim.

Thirty minutes later he was in the Gare de Lyon talking to the officials.

They informed him, confirming what he had been told at the hotel, that the Sheikh had left for Marseilles. He had travelled in a private Car which had been attached to the morning express.

"The *morning* express?" the Marquis queried.

"*Oui, Monsieur*. It departed at nine-thirty."

"You are quite certain the Sheikh was on it?"

"Quite certain, *Monsieur!* In fact, I saw him off myself."

The Marquis was silent. Then another official who had just entered the Station Master's room said:

"Another private coach chartered by the Sheikh was attached to the midday express, which has only just left."

"Who was on it?" the Marquis asked sharply.

"A number of Arabs, *Monsieur*, who were conveying a dead body."

"What exactly do you mean by that?"

"A coffin travelled with them, Milord."

"A coffin?"

The Marquis knew as he spoke that he was repeating what had been said in a rather foolish manner.

"You are quite certain you saw a coffin?" he insisted.

"Of course, Milord."

"And there was no woman with them? She might have been wearing a *burnous* and a *litham*, as if she was an Arab."

"No woman, Milord, only six men and a coffin."

The Marquis thought for a moment. Then he said sharply:

"I want to hire a special train to take me to Marseilles as swiftly as it is humanly possible to get there!"

*   *   *

To Kitrina the journey seemed endless.

There was no question of her being able to escape.

The Arabs kept coming to the door of her bedroom to see if she was there, and after they had been travelling for an hour they brought her some food and mint tea.

She drank the tea, and because she still felt so weak she attempted to eat a little of the food, although she found it almost impossible to swallow.

All she could think of was what would be waiting for her when she reached Algiers where by listening to what the Arabs were saying she learned was where they were going.

"He'll be waiting for us in Algiers," one of them said, and there was no question who 'he' was.

She guessed that the Sheikh had gone ahead, rather than travel with her, because it would be humiliating for him if she tried to defy him or fought against him in front of his followers.

She was aware that like all Arab Sheikhs he was fiercely proud not only as the Ruler of a tribe, but also of his masculinity among the women in his *Harem*.

He was used to women who kissed his feet adoringly and considered it an honour and a privilege to be one of his concubines, let alone his wife.

She therefore knew that the Sheikh would see her first in private.

She wondered frantically if there was anything she could say or do which would make him release her, either because he did not want her or else because he was unexpectedly merciful.

Then she remembered the fire in his eyes and knew that quite certainly he would make her his, as he had said he intended to do.

Kitrina was very innocent and had no real idea of how a man made love to a woman.

But she knew that to be touched by the Sheikh or to be kissed by him would be a degradation so horrible and so frightening to contemplate that all she could think of was that somehow she must die before it happened.

Once again she was desperately wondering how she could manage to kill herself, unless perhaps she could pull one of the knives from his belt and before he could prevent her, plunge it into her breast.

There was a place, she knew, just above the ribs which her father had once said was a most vulnerable spot. A man or woman, if pierced there by the point of a knife, would die instantly.

'Why did I not ask him exactly where it was?' Kitrina thought now.

And yet she was sure when the moment came his hand would guide her and she would die before the Sheikh could make her his wife.

Then as the train steamed on she felt that if the Marquis kissed her it would be for her the most perfect and wonderful thing that could possibly happen.

He must have kissed so many women, and she was sure that they had never forgotten what must have been to each one of them a rapturous experience.

He was so handsome and overwhelmingly attractive, and she knew now he was the man she had always envisaged in her dreams, who had been a mixture of her father and all the heroes she had read about in the History Books at Convent.

Until now her dream-man had never had a face.

He had been tall, dark and handsome, and had talked to her in the same deep voice which the Marquis had used to her just before he left her in the Bois and she had been spirited away from him.

Now she knew that the man she wanted to love, and who could make her as happy as her father and mother had been, was the Marquis.

'If only he had kissed me once,' she thought, 'it would be something to think about as I die.'

Now all she had to remember was his kindness, and her feeling of comfort and security when, as they had driven away from Celeste's house she had slipped her hand into his and felt his fingers close over hers.

"I love him! I love him!" she whispered, and the wheels beneath her seemed to rumble the same words over and over again.

Despite her feeling of helplessness and the logic which told her that the Marquis, even when he guessed where she had been taken, would not be in time to save her, Kitrina hoped that perhaps by some miracle he would be waiting for her at Marseilles.

Yet when the Arabs made her lie down again in the coffin, she knew it was such a forlorn hope it was pointless to think about it.

"If you lie still I'll not tie you up," the Head man said, "but we have to gag you in case you scream."

"I cannot move in such a small space, so please leave me free," Kitrina begged.

Because she did not want them to touch her she got into the coffin without any protest.

When they tied the handkerchief which she thought was not very clean, over her mouth, she put her head down on a small white satin pillow which matched the lining of the rest of the coffin.

She was relieved that they did not put on the lid until a few minutes before the train entered the terminus, and she saw what she had not noticed before – a wreath of white flowers which was placed in the centre of the coffin-lid, presumably to impress the on-lookers.

It was very early in the morning when they arrived at Marseilles and there was only a faint light coming through the holes in the coffin as Kitrina was carried down the platform.

Then there was a carriage, or perhaps a hearse, she was not certain which, to take her with her Arab body-guard from the station to the Quay.

It had all been cleverly thought out, because as she knew, neither shipowners nor railway managers really liked conveying coffins.

She guessed that she was being taken onto the Steamer which would carry her from Marseilles to Algiers before any passengers could see it and feel superstitious because they were travelling with a dead body.

She had the idea that it was usual for a coffin to be put down in the hold.

At least she was saved that, and as she was carried into one of the two cabins that were on the main deck of the ship she heard one of the ship's Officers asking the Arabs to make sure that the blinds were drawn over the port-holes and the door was kept closed.

"We will do that," the Head man said in his bad French.

"And you'll not be able to disembark until all the other passengers are ashore," the Officer continued sharply. "I suppose you have some conveyance waiting for you?"

"Yes, yes," the Arab replied. "Everything has been arranged."

Satisfied, the ship's Officer left them alone, and when he had gone the Arabs unscrewed the lid of the coffin and peeped inside to see if Kitrina was all right.

"I am alive," she said before they could ask the question. "But it is difficult for me to breathe."

"You must stay there until the ship leaves," the Head man said. "Then I will let you move, but if you try to leave the cabin, I will tie you up and beat you! Do you understand?"

He was only threatening her, Kitrina knew, because he was frightened.

She was quite sure he would not lay a finger on her in

case she complained to the Skeikh.

She said however:

"I will not try to escape, but please, as soon as you can, let me out. I have cramp in both my legs."

The Arab was sympathetic. At the same time, he was far too nervous to let her move out of the coffin until the ship had sailed.

But they left her face uncovered, ready, Kitrina knew, to put the lid back on again if anyone should knock on the door.

Because they were trying in their own way to be kind, they asked her what she would like to drink and fetched her some biscuits that were more palatable than the food they were eating themselves.

They tried to explain once again they were only obeying the Sheikh's orders.

She knew that their politeness came entirely from the fact that they were impressed by her future position as Chief Wife, and were afraid she might make trouble for them.

At the same time she was grateful for small mercies, and depressed with a misery which increased every mile they travelled across the sea which took her further and further from the Marquis.

Now she began to think despairingly that by now he would have accepted the inevitable, knowing that he could not save her without starting a private war against the Sheikh.

Even if he attempted in any way to rescue her, once she was officially married she was certain every Diplomat of England, France and Morocco would advise him that they could not interfere.

Besides, once she belonged to the Sheikh and was his possession – his woman – who would want her?

Kitrina felt during the voyage across to Africa that she was in a hell that exceeded anything she had ever read about or imagined.

At the same time, she thought, she grew up.

She was no longer a child, but a woman – a woman

suffering not only because she was afraid, but also because she was in love.

Every minute of the day her love for the Marquis had grown stronger and stronger.

She could only wonder how she had been so blind as not to realise when she was with him how much she loved him, and how he filled her whole life to the exclusion of everything else.

Now she could understand what her father had said when he told her that love was more important than anything else in the whole world.

Now she could understand why he and her mother had defied their relatives and the conventions in which they had been brought up, and had been prepared to live in exile rather than lose each other.

'That was love . . real love,' Kitrina told herself. 'It is the love I have for the Marquis, and the way nobody will . . ever love . . me.'

She felt the tears come into her eyes, but she would not let them fall.

She was past crying, past screaming, past even fighting against fate.

She just knew that she had found love and lost it, and that unless she could die she would suffer agonizingly with every breath she drew.

'I love you! I love you!' she was saying with her mind, her heart, and her soul.

She did not see the Arabs sitting cross-legged on the floor of the cabin or hear the laughter and chatter of the passengers on the deck outside.

All she could see was the Marquis's handsome face and hear the deep note in his voice as he said:

"I cannot lose you!"

At the same time, he had lost her! So now, she thought, he would forget her and would go back to England to his house, his vast estates and his relatives.

Then he would marry somebody suitable and of whom they approved.

If he ever thought of her again it would only be

because somebody had mentioned her father and how disgracefully he had behaved.

'He . . will forget . . me,' she whispered in her heart.

Then she knew that the agony she was suffering was more intense and more violent than anything she would suffer at the hands of the Shiekh.

Chapter Six

When night came the Arabs, at Kitrina's request, left her alone in the cabin so that she could wash before she lay down on the only bed.

She was well aware they were standing sentinel outside the door, and it would be impossible for her to escape.

Even if she somehow attracted the attention of one of the passengers, she was certain that before she could make her predicament known, the Arabs would in some way make certain that her cry for help was unheeded.

'There is nothing I can do,' she told herself miserably.

She felt that every throb of the ship's engines carried her further and further away from the Marquis.

She thought that the Steamer in which they were travelling seemed a slow one, and at one period the Mediterranean was so rough that the Arabs kept leaving the cabin because they were seasick.

But this was no help for her, and she turned her face away from them and tried to sleep.

But all she could think of was the Marquis, and how happy they had been together in Paris, and how she had managed to make him laugh.

'I love him! I love him!' was all she could say over and over again, until even to herself the three words became monotonous.

Then she lay thinking that somehow she must kill herself and whether it would be best to try to make one wild rush into the sea.

Yet she had the idea that if she threw herself overboard there would be some officious seaman ready to dive in to rescue her, and her position would be even worse than before.

She found herself remembering all she had seen of Arab

Harems when she had travelled with her father.

It was a long time ago, and she had been very young, but she could remember the women lying about on plushly covered sofas, who had seemed to have nothing to do but eat, sleep, and chatter amongst themselves.

It was a life, she thought, that was absolutely alien to that which she had spent with her father and mother, or the happy hours she had enjoyed with the Marquis in Paris.

'Whether I die by my own hand or have to live in some *Harem* is immaterial,' she thought, 'because living such a life I should be dead to everything that matters.'

When morning came the Arabs brought her food and black coffee which she thought gave her the strength to keep on concentrating on what she could do.

She knew they were steaming nearer and nearer to Algiers and what she really feared was seeing again the passionate look of lust in the Sheikh's eyes.

He made her feel as if he was physically touching her, even though they were standing apart from each other.

She knew that he terrified her and that the thought of being his wife was something so horrible, so unspeakably revolting, that she wanted to scream and go on screaming.

But she knew if she made the slightest sound the Arabs would gag her and put her in the coffin which lay waiting on the floor, and screw down the lid.

'I must do something!' she told herself.

But it was impossible to think what she could do, without the risk of being handled violently by the men sitting around her cross-legged on the floor.

They were playing cards, but she knew that all the time they were acutely aware of her. At her slightest movement their faces turned towards her just in case she was contemplating something which would bring down upon them the wrath of the Sheikh.

The long hours of the day passed unbearably slowly.

Then when the sun had lost some of its heat and was sinking low on the horizon the Arabs began to chatter amongst themselves and pull aside the curtains over the port-holes and she knew land must be in sight.

She thought then that perhaps the Steamer had been faster than she had imagined and they had reached Algiers more quickly than she had expected.

It had certainly taken longer the last time she had crossed the Mediterranean, but then she had been in what she knew was a very old ship, and she had certainly not been able to afford the comfort of a cabin.

Besides at that time she had been much distressed at her mother's death and was also terrified, as she was now, of the Sheikh. The passage had seemed interminably slow until she stepped ashore at Marseilles and thought that having reached France she would be safe, as least from him.

But she had been mistaken.

He had found her again in Paris, and she wished now she had never gone to the Opera with the Marquis where he had seen her.

Perhaps if she had not done so she would have been able to remain in obscurity, and the Sheikh would have assumed he had lost her for ever.

But wishes did not put back the clock.

He had seen her, had been determined she would not escape him again, and had won.

The Arabs were chatting excitedly, pointing out, she thought, the places they knew in the town above the harbour.

After some minutes they turned to her and she knew this was the moment when she was expected to climb back into the coffin.

They again tied a handkerchief over her mouth, and as she lay down they understood she did not want them to assist her or touch her.

For one moment she felt a sudden panic sweep through her, and if the gag had not been over her mouth she would have screamed.

Yet even as she had the impulse to struggle against

being shut away from the light and air, the coffin-lid came down sharply over her face and she heard the Arabs screwing it into place.

Then there was a slight thud and she thought they must have replaced the now fading wreath of flowers on the top. Then she heard them hurrying once again to the port-holes.

She tried not to listen, she tried not to think, but shut her eyes and prayed that somehow her father would help her find a way to die.

Although he had been very fond of many of the Arabs with whom he was close friends, she knew he would be shocked and horrified at the idea of her being one of the Sheikh's wives and being incarcerated for the rest of her life in his *Harem*.

'Save me, Papa! Save me!' she cried.

Then there was the sound overriding everything else of the Steamer drawing alongside the Quay and she envisaged the people aboard waving to their friends who would be waiting for them, and the porters ready to come aboard to carry off the luggage.

There would be the usual excitement and commotion which always happened in any harbour when a ship docked.

The Arabs were talking excitedly and she wondered if the Sheikh would meet them on the Quay or whether he would have her coffin carried to some house in the town.

She was certain from what she knew of the Arabs in the past that this was what would happen. He would be waiting for her in one of those houses which looked so unimportant from the outside.

Inside there would be a maze of small courtyards, cool passages, and dim rooms where women peeped out through lattice-covered windows.

She imagined him waiting for her with that passionate look in his eyes which made her so frightened.

Perhaps he would be sitting cross-legged on a pile of cushions and she would be brought before him like a slave who had been captured in war.

She knew he was not the sort of man with whom she could talk on equal terms or try to bargain with for her freedom.

She wished she was a man and could fight him physically. Even if she died in the attempt, at least she would have had the satisfaction of knowing she had been brave enough to defy him.

But again she knew this was only wishful thinking, and there was nothing left for her to do now but pray desperately, despairingly, knowing how ineffectual her prayers must be.

Suddenly there was the sound of the cabin-door opening and somebody speaking sharply and authoritatively in French.

It was difficult to hear what was being said, but she thought the Arabs were protesting volubly about something, although she could not understand what it was.

Then to her astonishment she heard the sound of the screws being removed from the coffin, and she feared she had been mistaken and it was not a Frenchman who was giving the orders, but the Sheikh himself.

Then as the lid was lifted off she kept her eyes shut for a moment, terrified of seeing his dark face.

Then almost as if she was compelled to do so, she looked up and it was the Marquis who was looking down at her.

*   *   *

The Marquis had in fact, been desperately afraid when he reached Marseilles and found that the Steamer on which six Arabs and a coffin were travelling had already left the harbour.

The special train in which he had travelled had been two hours behind the Express which carried Kitrina.

Although he pushed it to move quicker and quicker with every nerve in his body, it had arrived in Marseilles too late to prevent Kitrina from being carried aboard the Steamer.

The Chief of Police in Paris had already telegraphed to his colleague in Marseilles, and the Marquis received all the information he required and was also given the assurance that even if he did not reach Algiers before the Steamer, Kitrina and her escort would be prevented from landing until the coffin had been investigated.

It was unlikely, even if the Sheikh was there, that he would be able to talk his way out of such a difficult situation.

It was, in fact, only by the greatest good fortune that the Marquis's yacht was in Marseilles and ready to put to sea.

He had ordered the Captain to sail to Monte Carlo which he intended to visit when it suited him.

However he had learnt when he reached Paris that the Captain, after passing through a violent storm in the Bay of Biscay, had put into Marseilles for a few minor repairs.

When he guessed that Kitrina was being taken to Marseilles he had telegraphed instructions for the *Sea Lion* to stay in harbour but to be ready to put to sea at a moment's notice.

The minute he learned from the Police that a Steamer had left for Algiers with a coffin aboard he hurried to the *Sea Lion* and told the Captain to make sure they reached Algiers in record time.

They had actually overtaken and passed the Steamer during the night, and the Marquis had wondered if he should propose to board the vessel rather than allow it to reach the coast of Africa.

It was obvious however that the Police were not anxious to have a scene with the Sheikh in public and he thought they would be reluctant to bring a case against him for kidnapping.

That was something the Marquis himself did not want either, thinking that, if it became known that he was in any way involved, the Press would undoubtedly make a sensational story of it, which would be extremely damaging to Kitrina.

He had no wish for the world to know she was the offspring of her father's scandalous elopement with the

Queen's Lady-in-Waiting, and he was determined that if possible, her link with the Elke family should not be divulged.

That would only make things more difficult than they were already.

In fact, it had crossed the Marquis's mind that if the Sheikh succeeded in carrying Kitrina away, she would never be heard of again.

In which case there would be no problem for him to solve, and no gossip to revive the story of Gerald Elke's and Lady Blyton's disgraceful behaviour.

But the thought of the Sheikh touching Kitrina and making her his so-called wife made the Marquis feel as if his whole being was on fire.

How dare an Arab kidnap a young girl with such bare-faced effrontery?

How dare he think he could treat any European woman in such a way and make her what was to all intents and purposes a slave?

Without being aware of it the Marquis clenched his hands until the nails of his fingers drove into the palms.

He knew then that he would kill the Arab, or any other man who hurt Kitrina and made her afraid as she had been when he had felt her whole body trembling against his.

'I have to save her!' he vowed.

He knew that whatever the cost of himself, or for that matter to the Elke family, he would do so.

The *Sea Lion* lived up the Ship-builder's expectations of her and arrived in Algiers harbour before midday.

"I'm certain, M'Lord," the Captain said proudly, "that we've created a new record!"

He was rather surprised, however, when the Marquis merely nodded his head and did not seem as elated by the information as he would have expected him to be.

He was, in fact, pre-occupied in looking ashore to see if the Chief of Police was there waiting for him.

To his relief the Chief was easily to be seen with several smartly uniformed *Gendarmes* with him.

The Marquis was important and impressive enough to

have things arranged exactly as he wanted them, which included keeping Kitrina's identity a secret.

The Chief of Police and his *Gendarmes* went aboard the Steamer after the majority of the passengers had disembarked.

As the Marquis knew, the coffin would be left until the last moment, so that none of the people who had made the voyage from Marseilles would be aware there was one on board.

When the Police opened the cabin-door, the Arabs had stared at them in horror and dismay, but the Marquis had eyes only for the coffin in the centre of the cabin, the faded wreath of white flowers on top of it.

As the Chief of Police gave the order for the lid to be unscrewed, he waited with a feeling of apprehension that was more painful than anything he had ever known in the whole of his life.

Supposing after all this he was mistaken and it was not Kitrina, as he suspected, lying in the coffin, but a genuinely dead Arab who was being brought back from Paris to his own land?

If that proved to be the case, he would have no idea where she might be, or what had happened to her, and in the meantime she might easily be married to the Sheikh and consigned to his *Harem* from which it would be impossible to rescue her.

He thought as the last screw was pulled out and the Arabs reluctantly started to raise the lid that it was the most tense moment of his whole life.

Then as he saw her pale hair spread out over the white cushion and the gag over her mouth, he felt as if the blood flowed back into his veins and he could breathe again.

She was there, but just for one terrifying second because her eyes were closed he thought she must be dead.

Then as she looked up at him and he saw a radiance transform her face, he knew that she was very much alive.

* * *

As she felt the Marquis carefully descending a companion-

112

way carrying her in his arms, Kitrina knew he was taking her down to a cabin.

For the first time since being taken from the Steamer, she opened her eyes.

Because she was so frightened she had in the last moments before their arrival felt as if the breath had left her body and she was drifting away into unconsciousness.

She thought perhaps she was suffocating and that would be an easier way to die than any other.

Then as the coffin-lid had been taken off and she felt the fresh air on her face, she had finally looked up to see the Marquis, and had known her prayers had been answered.

He had bent down, lifted her up out of the coffin and somebody had untied the knot on the gag at the back of her head.

As it was taken away she made a little murmur and hid her face against the Marquis's shoulder.

She felt him carrying her away, and had known that now nothing else mattered because he was there and had saved her.

She did not want to speak, she did not want to ask any questions; she only knew that her nightmare was over, she was close to him, and she thought she could feel his heart beating against hers.

He carried her easily and she wondered vaguely where they were going but knew that it did not matter.

Then she had the idea that they were walking slowly down a gang-plank.

She could hear the sound of people talking and chattering but it all seemed very far away, and all that mattered was the Marquis holding her against him, and she was alive, safe, and with him.

The Marquis carried her some distance, and then there was another gang-plank and the sound of his footsteps on a deck as he spoke to somebody in English.

Then they were going down some steps and she knew without looking or being told that they were in a cabin.

It was then for the first time that the Marquis spoke to her.

"You are all right?" he asked. "Those devils have not hurt you?"

His voice seemed to penetrate through the mist of happiness which enveloped her because she was in his arms.

She opened her eyes to look up at him and found his face very near to hers.

She stared at him for a moment. Then she said:

"I . . I thought . . I would have to . . k . kill myself!"

It was then as if the sound of her own voice released the tension and the terror which had pervaded her for so long, and she burst into tears.

As she reached out her hands to hold onto the Marquis she cried tempestuously.

She cried against his shoulder, quite unable to control the tears which seemed to come from the very depths of her soul.

"It is all right," the Marquis said soothingly, "it is all over, and I promise you that this shall never happen again!"

"I . . I . . prayed and . . p . prayed," Kitrina wept, "b . but . . I did not . . think you . . would be able to . . s . save me."

"But I have saved you," he said gently. "You are safe – completely safe. I know how terrifying it must have been, but now it is over."

Kitrina's tears abated a little and she managed to whisper:

"P . perhaps . . he will . . try again."

"I will make very sure he does not!" the Marquis promised.

"You are here! You are . . really here!" Kitrina said as if it was something she found it hard to believe.

She looked up at him as she spoke and he saw the tears on her cheeks and her eyelashes wet above the blue of her eyes.

He thought that no-one could look so young, so adorable, and at the same time so pathetic.

"You are safe," he said quietly. "I promise that you are safe!"

Very gently he put her down on the bed in the cabin, then sitting beside her he said:

"I think what you should do now is have a bath. I want you to try the new and what I feel is a very original one which I have recently installed in my yacht. Afterwards we will have dinner together, and you can tell me everything that has happened to you! Then I will tell you how I broke the record to get here and save you."

He smiled at her as he spoke and Kitrina reached out her arms to ask:

"How can you be so . . marvellous as to . . save me like . . Perseus saving Andromeda?"

"I think really he had an easier task," the Marquis laughed, "but I am glad you think I am like Perseus."

"Only much . . much more . . wonderful!" Kitrina said. "I . . I thought you would never . . guess what had h . . happened to me."

"I am rather hurt that you should underestimate my intelligence!" the Marquis said.

Kitrina knew he was teasing her and while the tears were still on her cheeks she managed to give him a little smile.

"I would love a bath," she said, "but . . I am afraid I have no other gown with me . . so you will have to put up with what I am wearing now."

"Tomorrow will be different," the Marquis promised. "When I left Paris in such a hurry, I sent a message for Hicks to follow me with my luggage and yours. He will be here on the next Steamer which arrives at dawn tomorrow morning."

Kitrina gave a little laugh.

"You think of everything!" she said.

"As it happens, I have been very busy thinking of you," he answered, "and I have also been very anxious."

There was a note in his voice that made her feel with a leap of her heart that he had really minded losing her.

She thought for a moment that he hesitated as if he was about to say something else before he added:

"I am going to fetch you a glass of champagne which I

115

think you need after all you have been through, and one of my stewards will prepare your bath for you. Afterwards, we shall have all the evening to talk to one another."

"That will be very . . exciting!" Kitrina cried.

At the same time, when she had bathed in what she knew was a very modern bath to be found in a yacht, she could not help wishing that she had something different to wear in place of the gown that was badly creased from being enclosed in the coffin, and which she had worn for what seemed to be a century of time.

It was therefore a surprise when she came from the bathroom, wrapped in a white towelling dressing-gown that was far too long for her, to see something strange lying on the bed in her cabin.

For the moment she did not know what it was.

Then there was a knock on the door and when she said: "Come in!" a Steward explained:

"His Lordship thought as you'd nothing with you to wear, Miss, you'd like to try on this kaftan. It's just been bought from one of the shops near the Quay."

"A kaftan!" Kitrina exclaimed with delight.

She remembered now how long ago her mother had bought several kaftans in a native Bazaar, and wore them occasionally in the evening to please her father.

He mother had looked very lovely in them and Kitrina knew that the one on the bed, which was a pale *Eau de Nile* silk embroidered round the neck and sleeves would certainly be more becoming than her creased gown in which she had spent the previous night.

"Thank you very much!" she said to the Steward. "Please tell His Lordship I will be with him as soon as I am dressed."

When she put on the kaftan she knew that the Marquis with his eyes for detail had guessed it would fit her almost exactly.

Because she knew that any arrangement of her hair would look wrong when she was wearing Arab dress, she merely parted her fair hair in the middle and combed it to fall in heavy waves on either side of her face.

She had to manage with a man's thin comb which she knew must have been borrowed from the Marquis.

But when she looked in the mirror she thought with her pretty kaftan and her fair hair she looked very feminine, and she hoped that she would please him.

She was however a little shy as she came from her cabin to find the Steward waiting to escort her to the Saloon where the Marquis was waiting.

It was very attractive with white panelling, and the sofas, chairs, and the curtains over the port-holes were of chintz with a pattern of exotic flowers and birds.

But Kitrina could see nothing but the Marquis looking extremely smart in what she knew was the conventional yachting dress for a man of white trousers with a blue blazer ornamented with gold buttons.

He looked at her with a faint smile on his lips and she ran towards him eagerly saying:

"How could you be so clever as to find me something to wear? I love my kaftan, and I had forgotten how pretty they are."

"I will buy you a much prettier one tomorrow," he replied, "but this was the best that could be found at a moment's notice in the nearest shop."

Kitrina gave a little sigh of happiness and sat down on the sofa.

"Am I really . . here," she asked, "and with . . you? I keep feeling that I shall . . wake up."

"You are awake," the Marquis said, "and you are to forget everything that has happened since the last time we saw each other in Paris, and that is an order!"

He spoke almost sharply, and Kitrina said meekly:

"I will try . . but I want to touch you . . just to be certain you are . . real."

She spoke in a way that a child might have done, but the Marquis drew in his breath.

Then when he might have said something to her, the door opened and the Stewards came in with dinner.

They moved to a table which was laid ready for them,

and although she had thought she would be too excited to eat, Kitrina found she was quite hungry.

She had not been able to eat anything that the Arabs had brought her, although she had drunk the coffee.

Now the delicious food which the Marquis seemed to have wherever he went was irresistible, and she ate a little of every dish and sipped the champagne he insisted on her drinking.

While the stewards were serving them they talked about everything except themselves.

When dinner was over and the Marquis sat back in his chair with a glass of brandy in his hand, Kitrina heard the engines starting up and looked at him questioningly.

"It is now dark," he said, "and we are going a little way down the coast because I want you to have a peaceful night, and not be disturbed early by the sounds that are inevitable if we remain in harbour."

"Are you . . thinking of . . me?" Kitrina asked.

"Of course I am thinking of you!" he replied. "You have made it impossible for me to think of anything else these last forty-eight hours, which have been an agony I hope never to experience again."

She looked away from him and he said:

"But I want you to rest, and then while we go anywhere in the Mediterranean that you wish, we can talk about ourselves and our future."

"At the moment I am very . . content with the . . present," Kitrina replied with a little tremor in her voice.

She was thinking as she spoke how at this moment she had expected to be in an Arab house with the Sheikh, or perhaps already taken away by him into the desert.

As if he knew what she was thinking, the Marquis said sharply:

"Forget it! I want you to think about us, Kitrina, you and me, and as that is a very big subject, I am now going to send you to bed."

He paused before he went on in a deep voice:

"Tomorrow, when the sun is shining and we are very happy to be together, we will talk about all the things that

I am sure are trembling on your lips, but which I think should wait until you are not so tired."

"I . . I expect you are . . right," Kitrina agreed. "Anyway, nothing matters except that I am here with you . . and I am safe . . really safe!"

"Really safe!" the Marquis confirmed.

The yacht was moving over the smooth water and Kitrina rose to her feet.

By the light of the candles on the table she looked very lovely. The kaftan clung to her figure, revealing the small curves of her breasts and outlining the slimness of her hips.

"I cannot imagine anything that could become you more," the Marquis said, as if he was following his own thoughts. "At the same time, when your clothes arrive tomorrow, I may change my mind and like you best in frills of Parisian lace, or a swirl of white chiffon that will make you look even more like an angel than you do at this moment!"

Kitrina laughed.

"You are being very poetic."

"Strangely enough, that is what I feel, Kitrina. That is what you have done to me."

She looked at him and somehow it was impossible to look away.

Then as if she suddenly felt shy she said quickly:

"I will do as . . you say, but I hope tomorrow comes . . very quickly, because there is so much I want to . . talk to you . . about."

She moved across the Saloon as she spoke. The Marquis did not rise, but merely sat in his chair watching her go.

When she finally vanished from sight he walked from the Saloon out onto the deck to watch the lights of Algiers fading into the distance.

He had told the Captain to go only a little way down the coast because, although he had not said so to Kitrina, he had made arrangements with his Lawyers in Paris to investigate the ownership of the Villa.

He had instructed them also to find out if her mother

had a Bank account in any of the Banks in Algiers.

While he had been waiting for the Steamer which carried Kitrina and the Arabs to arrive, he had had a short conversation with the Solicitor in charge of the investigation.

He was told that, as he had guessed, the *Comte* de Villeneuve, having completed his term of office as Governor of Senegal, had been offered a more important post in French North Africa.

He had therefore bought the Villa in Algiers where he intended to live with Kitrina's mother.

This would account, the Marquis understood, for the fact that he had died at the Villa.

There was however a great deal more he wanted to find out, but most of all to discover if there was any money for Kitrina to inherit.

He gave instructions to the Solicitor to carry out his investigations as quickly as possible, then forgot about it in his anxiety as to whether or not he would find Kitrina on the Steamer, for there was always the possibility that he might have been wrong in his assumption that the Sheikh was conveying her to Africa in a very clever and unexpected manner.

However now his trouble was over, and there were only a few loose ends to be tied up with regard to Algiers before they could steam away and forget the place ever existed.

There was however, one problem still unsolved; that of Kitrina.

He stood on deck feeling the soft warm fragrant air against his face.

The heat of the day had gone and now there was just a very faint breeze from the sea.

It was very quiet and beautiful, and he wished that Kitrina was beside him.

Then as the yacht came to a standstill in a small bay and the anchor went down, he was aware that they were only a very short distance from the shore.

He wanted Kitrina to watch the stars overhead

becoming more and more brilliant until it seemed as if the sky was filled with diamonds and the light of them was reflected dazzlingly in the waters below.

It was so lovely that he had a sudden yearning for her which he could not ignore.

He knew as it swept over him that he needed her, for while she was in many ways a child, she was also a very desirable woman.

He was too experienced not to know that Kitrina loved him; that her eyes were filled with dazzling light when she looked at him and there was a little tremor in her voice when she thanked him for anything.

And yet he was aware that she was completely un-awakened to the fire and rapture of love that could exist between a man and a woman, and he thought that to teach her would be the most exciting thing he had ever done in his whole life.

He remembered how Celeste had said it was important for a woman to be taught by a man who was gentle and tender when she first learnt about love.

He told himself that was what he would be, and he would make sure that Kitrina experienced the spiritual ecstasy which was very different from the sensuous passion that was aroused like a raging fire by two sophisticated lovers.

'She is very young, very pure and very idealistic,' the Marquis said to himself, 'and I must be very controlled.'

He knew as he spoke that the blood was throbbing in his temples, and he felt as if his breath was constricted in his throat, while his heart was beating tumultuously.

'I want her!' he told himself, 'God, how I want her! Celeste was right – I must protect and look after her as no one else could do.'

He looked up at the stars and felt as he did so that Kitrina was with him.

He thought whimsically that he should pull the stars from the sky and place them like a halo on her pale hair.

'She is unique,' he said to the night, 'and Fate has brought her to me! Who am I to deny Fate?'

He felt as if he was excusing himself and his actions to some power which had the authority to question him.

Then he laughed as if at his own imagination and took one more look at the stars above him, before he walked from the deck down into the quiet darkness below it.

Chapter Seven

When Kitrina reached her cabin she found lying on the bed a thin white nightgown.

It was made of cheap, almost transparent material and decorated with slightly coarse lace, but she knew it was the only type that could have been bought in the shops around the Quay and was very grateful to the Marquis for thinking of it.

As she took off her pretty kaftan and hung it up in a cupboard set in the cabin wall, she thought that no man could be so considerate or so understanding of a woman's needs.

Then with a little stab of her heart she knew the explanation was that there had been so many women in his life!

How, she asked herself, was it possible for him to be interested in her after the beautiful ladies she had seen fawning on him in Paris?

At the same time, he had saved her, she was now with him again, they were on his yacht, and nothing could be more marvellous.

She put on the thin nightgown thinking it was exactly what she needed in the heat of North Africa. Then she got into bed.

She did not however, turn out the light, feeling afraid that in the darkness she would imagine herself back in the coffin, being carried to the Sheikh from whom she would never be able to escape.

As she lay looking at the attractive cabin with its painted walls and soft blue curtains, she thought that no one could be so lucky as she was.

"Thank You, God!" she said, "I am sure it was Papa who told You how desperate I was, and how there seemed to be no alternative for me but to die."

Now she wanted to live and she felt the hours could not pass quickly enough until it was tomorrow and she could see the Marquis again.

She was thinking of him and felt as if her whole body was throbbing with her feeling for him when the door opened and he came in.

She looked up and her eyes shone as if from a thousand candles inside her as the Marquis walked across the cabin and sat down on the side of the bed facing her.

He was wearing a blue robe which touched the floor and the frill of his nightshirt was very white against his skin.

Kitrina put out her hands towards him.

"I . . I was thinking of . . you," she said, "and now . . you have come to say goodnight to me . . and it makes everything more . . perfect that it is . . already."

Looking at her the Marquis thought no one could look so adorable, so childlike, and at the same time, so utterly desirable.

Her eyes seemed very blue in her small face and her hair had only a touch of gold in contrast to the whiteness of the pillows.

"I am glad you think it is perfect to be here with me," he said in a deep voice, "and that it what I want to talk to you about, Kitrina."

Her hand was in his and he felt her fingers give a little quiver, as if what he had said was exciting.

Following his thoughts he went on;

"I was, of course, desperately worried about you when you were taken from me in Paris, and I am deeply concerned for your future. What is more important than anything else is that you should be safe."

"I am . . safe with . . you."

"That is what I hoped you would say," he answered, "and what I am going to suggest to you, Kitrina, is . . ."

He paused as if he was trying to find the right words with which to express himself.

Then unexpectedly there was a knock at the door.

The Marquis turned his head.

"What is it?" he asked sharply.

Almost before he could say the words the door opened and one of the Officers stood there.

"Excuse me, M'Lord, but the Captain says Your Lordship should know that he thinks we're about to be attacked."

"Attacked?" the Marquis exclaimed.

He rose to his feet as he spoke and as he walked towards the door Kitrina gave a little cry.

It was like the cry of a child or a small animal that has been caught in a trap and the Marquis paused.

"Stay here!" he said firmly.

Then he was gone and the door closed behind him.

With a cry of sheer terror Kitrina buried her face in the pillow and pulled the sheet over her head.

Outside the door the Marquis said to the Officer:

"What is it?"

"The seaman on watch, M'Lord, reports seeing what he thinks are Arabs up on cliff and in the bay. They've been watching us, and the Captain is sure they intend to board us by force."

As he was speaking the Marquis had gone into his own cabin and pulling off his robe was slipping into a pair of black trousers and the lawn shirt he had worn at dinner.

He took a silk scarf from the drawer, tied it round his neck and, still wearing his velvet slippers embroidered with his insignia in gold thread, he hurried up the companionway.

As he expected, the Captain was on the bridge and with him were two other Officers.

The Marquis noticed that while he had already ordered all the lights on deck to be extinguished, the light of the stars made it easy to see there were men silhouetted against the sky and others descending in what seemed to be a surreptitious manner down the side of the cliff onto the beach of the bay.

The Marquis had taken with him from his cabin his revolver which he had been carrying when he rescued

Kitrina from the Steamer. It was the very latest model and a six-shooter.

He saw the Captain and the other Officers all had revolvers in their hands and he asked;

"How many men aboard can fire a rifle?"

"Ten of them are crack shots, M'Lord," the Captain replied, "the rest are problematical, but determined, if the need arises, to have a go!'

"Good!" the Marquis said.

He then saw what he had not noticed as he came on the bridge that a number of men were lying on the side of the deck which faced the bay in a way which would make it impossible for them to be seen from the shore.

It would enable them to fire at an enemy while being protected by the foot of the railings which encircled the deck.

"We will do nothing unless they attack us first," the Marquis said taking command.

As he spoke he was aware that the Captain, who had been with him on his previous yacht, and with whom he had in the past, been in some very tight spots from aggressive tribesmen or pirates, had already taken every precaution.

He had never expected that on this cruise, on which he had intended only to go to Monte Carlo, he would need the quite large armoury he always carried on his yachts.

As the whim took him, he would steam up the Amazon at a moment's notice, or infiltrate into some of the lesser-known rivers of Africa or other parts of the world, and it was always wise to be well armed.

He thought now this was something he had not imagined could happen, and yet he might have known the Sheikh would not acknowledge defeat so quickly.

It was obvious that his desire for Kitrina was a challenge to his pride and his authority, and he was not expecting an English yacht-owner to be aggressive or capable of fighting what was clearly a considerable number of his tribe.

Then as the Marquis watched from the darkness of the bridge, he realised what the Sheikh intended to do.

Some of his men were already moving towards the water's edge preparatory to wading or swimming to board the yacht as quickly as they could.

If there was any opposition, they would be covered by gun-fire from the men on top of the cliffs who would be able to see any movement on deck.

It was quite a clever plan so long as the Sheikh was right in his assumption that those on board would be off their guard and the majority by this time of the night, asleep.

Anchored near the shore with its lights, the *Sea Lion* looked very peaceful and defenceless.

Then as the first men began to enter the water the Marquis knew that they must be stopped.

He moved forward to the open door of the bridge.

"I will fire a warning shot over their heads," he said. "If they return the fire, then they must get what is coming to them."

As he spoke he fired his revolver into the air and the shot seemed to explode out into the stillness of the night and echo round the bay.

Instantly there was answering fire from the Arabs lying flat on top of the cliffs.

As it came the Marquis gave his orders to the men directly below him to commence firing.

"Fire!"

It was only with the greatest effort that they had restrained themselves until now, and their rifles picked out the men entering the water one by one.

As they fell a number of those on the top of the cliffs came scurrying down the path to the shore, shouting their battle-cry.

At the same time those left behind went on firing, and now there were 'no holds barred'.

The Captain and his Officers joined the Marquis in firing from the bridge, while there was no pause in the deliberate and accurate firing from the men lying on the deck.

It was then that the Marquis saw silhouetted against the stars a majestic figure which he knew to be the Sheikh.

He defied danger as he urged on his men, despite the opposition they had not expected.

Just for a moment the Marquis paused, then when he would have fired at him, a rifle bullet hit the Sheikh.

He staggered, throwing up his arms as he did so, and fell slowly backwards.

The men around him stopped firing, and as if what had happened was communicated in some way to those in the bay below, those of the Arabs who were not shot dead or drowned by the water in which they fell gradually retreated.

It was a pathetic progress as first one man then another was picked off by the seamen's rifles until the Marquis's voice rang out with the command;

"Cease fire!"

There were just two shots after he had spoken, then silence and everybody on deck watched the Arabs hurrying to safety, dragging one or two of their wounded with them, leaving a number behind.

Then as they gradually disappeared from view and were no longer silhouetted against the sky the Marquis said:

"Start the engines, Captain, and move a little further down the coast where we can spend a peaceful night."

He did not wait for affirmation or see the cheerful grins on the seamen's faces as they knew what a victory they had won.

Instead he walked quickly down to Kitrina's cabin.

He knew of how terrified she must have been and that the noise of the firing must have been unbearable when she had to listen to it without knowing what was happening.

He only paused at the door of his own cabin to put down his empty revolver, then as he opened the door of Kitrina's she flung herself against him.

She had, he knew, obeyed his command to stay where she was, however agonizing it was to be left alone.

He could feel her body trembling all over as she clung to him, apparently speechless with fear.

"It is all right," he said. "They are defeated, and they will never trouble us again."

"B . but . . he will . . never give up."

The words were incoherent and hardly above a whisper, but the Marquis heard them.

She had flung back her head to speak and with her fair hair falling over her almost bare shoulders, her body showing through her diaphanous nightgown, she looked very lovely.

The Marquis looked at her for a long moment before he picked her up in his arms, carried her to the bed and laid her down on it.

As he expected her eyes were dilated with terror.

"It is all over," he said very quietly, "and the Sheikh will never bother you again. He is dead!"

For a moment she just stared at him wildly, before with a little murmur she hid her face against his shoulder, and while she still was trembling, he knew it was easier for her to breathe.

"Yes, he is dead," the Marquis repeated, "and you need never think of him again."

"You . . s . said I would be . . s . safe," she said like a child who feels a promise has not been fulfilled.

"I know," he agreed, "and it was very foolish of me to underestimate the enemy. But I cannot allow you ever again to be frightened by a Sheikh or by any other man, and I therefore want to know, my darling, how soon you will marry me!"

He thought as he spoke that his voice sounded strange even to himself.

Yet he knew that this was what he had to say and it was the only real solution to the problem of Kitrina.

Whatever the difficulties, whatever the repercussions from his family, she belonged to him, and there was no other way to ensure that she would not in the future be frightened as she was now.

Then slowly, almost as if she was afraid to move, Kitrina raised her face to his.

She looked at him for a long moment before she said in

a very small voice that seemed to come from a long distance:

"Did . did you . . did you . . really ask me to . . m . marry you?"

"I love you, Kitrina!" the Marquis answered. "And I think, my precious little one, that you love me."

"I love you . . until you . . fill my whole world," she replied, "but . . I never thought . . I never dreamt . . that you would m . marry me!"

She drew in her breath, then asked:

"You . . mean it . . you . . really mean it?"

"I mean it," the Marquis said firmly, "and I think, my sweet, we will be very happy together."

"*I* will be happy," Kitrina averred, "because it will be like being in . . Heaven to be always with you . . but . . you are sure . . quite sure . . that you think I am . . beautiful enough to be your . . wife?"

The Marquis's eyes were very tender as he said;

"I cannot imagine that anybody could be more beautiful! But there is more to my love than that. You belong to me, Kitrina, and have done so ever since we first met, and I know now that my life would not be complete without you."

"You . . feel that . . really and . . t . truly?"

"Really and truly!"

Then as if there was no need for words he bent his head and his lips found hers.

As he kissed her he knew that this was what he had been waiting for for a very long time, and it had been hopeless to try to fight against it.

The softness of her lips, the thrill that ran through her at his touch, gave him sensations that were different from anything he had ever felt before from any other woman.

There was something so pure, so angelic about Kitrina that, as he had thought on deck, he would be very gentle and tender with her.

He held her closer still and went on kissing her until she gave a little cry and hid her face against his neck.

"What is it , my precious?" he asked. "I am not frightening you?"

"You could . . never frighten me," she said. "It is . . just that . . when you kiss me . . it is like . . being amongst the stars . . and hearing the . . angels sing."

"That is what I want you to feel."

"I . . love you . . I love . . you!" Kitrina said. "B . but . . I still cannot understand . . h . how you can love me."

"I will make you sure that I love you when we are married," the Marquis said, "but now, my precious little angel, I think you should go to sleep because you have been through a very difficult and frightening time, and I want you to rest."

"I . . I do not . . want you to . . l . leave me."

The Marquis smiled as he knew that in her innocence she did not realise what she was asking.

He kissed her forehead before he said:

"As soon as we are married, that will never happen, but now I want you to try to sleep. If you are frightened, you have only to call out, and I will come to you."

"C. could you . . l . leave my . . d . door open?"

"Of course," The Marquis answered, "and mine will be open too. Once the ship is at anchor again, I will hear the slightest sound you make."

Because she had been so bemused by the Marquis's kisses, Kitrina did not realise that the engines had started up and the yacht was moving.

"Where are we going?" she asked.

"Only a little further down the coast."

The Marquis knew that by the morning the Arabs would have taken away most of their dead but he had no wish for Kitrina to see what was always an horrific sight – the aftermath of a battle.

"We will be . . safe?" she asked.

"Very, very safe," the Marquis promised, "and this time, my promise will be fulfilled, and there will be no further interruptions to our happiness."

"And . . I will really be your . . wife?"

"As soon as it is possible to arrange it," the Marquis

promised. "Perhaps tomorrow, if that will not be too soon."

"I . . I wish it could be . . tonight."

The Marquis smiled.

"I think anybody who could perform the Marriage Service would be asleep at this hour, and I feel too you would like to wait for Hicks to arrive with your gowns rather than be married in a kaftan."

"I . . I would not mind what I wore . . so long as I could be married to you."

Then before he could speak she added;

"At the same time . . I want . . you to think I . . look pretty."

The Marquis knew she was comparing herself with the ladies she had seen in Paris and he said;

"Every time I look at you, my lovely one, I think you look more beautiful than you did the last time, and tomorrow, I shall be able to tell you how beautiful you are and how much you mean to me."

He knew as he spoke that he was speaking with a sincerity that he had never used to any woman in the past.

Then as if it was easier to express his feelings with kisses, he kissed Kitrina again until she was breathless.

Then he laid her back against the pillows and pulled the sheet up to her chin, saying:

"Go to sleep. We have both had enough excitement for tonight, and I want you to look lovely tomorrow in the sunshine."

She looked up at him and he thought the expression in her eyes was so radiant that it would have been impossible for any artist however talented to depict it on canvas.

Then he kissed her hand and moved across the cabin to prop the door open with a chair.

As he did so he realised that the engines were slowing down until a few seconds later they were silent and he heard the anchor being let down.

"Goodnight, my precious wife-to-be," he said from the door.

With an effort he went to his own cabin.

132

When he reached it he could hardly believe the elation and happiness he felt within himself was not just a figment of his imagination.

He had never believed it possible that he could be in love so completely and overwhelmingly as he was at this moment.

He knew that it was because his love had been there even though he did not know it, and it had been impossible to suggest to Kitrina that he should have any other position in her life except that of her husband.

He had learnt that nothing mattered except her peace of mind and happiness, and he would fight and protect and guard her for the rest of their lives.

"How could I have known, how could I have guessed when I received Celeste's letter," he asked, " that Kitrina could alter my entire life?"

*　　*　　*

When Kitrina awoke, she knew it was later than she had expected and the noise outside the yacht told her that while she was still sleeping they had moved back into the harbour.

She felt even more surprised when Hicks came into the room to pull back the curtains over the port-hole and put a breakfast tray down beside her bed.

" Mornin', Miss!" he said, "I expect you're glad to see me, as I've brought all your pretty dresses for you."

Kitrina sat up and smiled at him.

"I am very, very glad to see you!"

"They're bringing the luggage down now," Hicks said, "and His Lordship says as soon as you're dressed and ready he wants to take you ashore."

When Hicks left, Kitrina hurried to have a bath, and by the time she had returned to the cabin, Hicks had extracted what he thought was one of her prettiest Parisian gowns and had put it ready on the bed.

It was white trimmed with real lace and there was a bonnet to go with it.

When she went upstairs to find the Marquis she knew by the expression in his eyes that he loved her.

She ran towards him, saying as she reached him:

"It is . . true . . what you said . . last night? I . . I did not . . dream it?"

"It is true," the Marquis confirmed, "and now, my darling, we are going ashore. We are to be married at *La Mairie* by the Mayor of Algiers."

Kitrina made a little murmur of excitement and he went on:

"I have discovered there is no Protestant Church here, so we are to be married French fashion, but when we get to Nice or Monte Carlo on the other side of the Mediterranean, we will have another wedding in Church. But I cannot wait for as long as that to make you my wife."

"I . . I am sure whatever way we are married . . God will bless us!"

"I know He will," the Marquis agreed.

A carriage was waiting for them and they drove up to the impressive building flying the French flag.

The Mayor, who was waiting for them, greeted the Marquis effusively and married them with all the pomp and ceremony of his Office, then insisted on drinking their health in champagne.

It was a very different wedding from what the Marquis had expected his would be like.

He had imagined there would be hundreds of guests, friends and relations, the Prince of Wales as the Guest of Honour, and the Queen represented by a distinguished Statesman.

And yet he thought now that nothing mattered except the happiness that seemed to radiate from Kitrina so that the French Officials seemed almost mesmerised by her, and their congratulations were spoken with a true sincerity.

Then as they drove away, the Mayor seeing them off, Kitrina slipped her hand into his and the Marquis knew how excited she was.

"I am . . yours!" she said in a breathless little voice.

"Mine!" the Marquis agreed. "We have only one more thing to do, my darling, before we leave Algiers, and then we need never come back."

"What . . is that?" Kitrina enquired.

"We are going to the Villa, which I have learnt was given to your mother by the *Comte* de Villeneuve, and which therefore is now yours."

"Mine?"

"Yes," the Marquis answered. "And because I feel you would never wish to live here, I think it would be best for you to sell it."

"Yes . . of course," Kitrina agreed.

"I have also learnt," the Marquis went on, "that there is some money in your mother's name in the Bank of Algiers, which will be transferred to you."

Kitrina's fingers tightened on his.

"Now I shall be able to give you a present," she said. "You have given me so many things, and I have wondered how I could ever say 'thank you'."

"I will solve that difficulty later," the Marquis said, "but of course my precious, I would love to have a present."

"Perhaps when we reach England I could give you something you really want," Kitrina said, "but you will have to help me choose it."

The Marquis did not reply that he had no intention of taking her to England for a long time.

He had already planned how it would be best to get his relatives over the shock of learning who he had married, but he was not quite certain of the best way to go about it.

Now he kissed Kitrina's fingers one by one as she wondered excitedly about what she could buy him, for instance a horse or even, if she could afford it, one of the new motor cars that were always being talked about in the newspapers.

The Marquis did not reply that he already had one at home and thought it a rather tiresome acquisition, much preferring his horses.

He knew the present he really wanted from Kitrina was herself.

To hold her in his arms and teach her about love would be a treasure beyond price, on which it would be impossible to set a value.

*   *   *

The Villa was situated high on the outskirts of the town and as they entered through the gate in the white wall that surrounded it, the Marquis saw that it was exceedingly beautiful.

There was a puzzled look on Kitrina's face as she said:

"I had almost forgotten how large it is! How could Mama have afforded to buy a house as big as this?"

"I expect," the Marquis said lightly, "the *Comte* gave it to her in gratitude for all the work she had done for him for so many years."

"Yes, of course . . that must have been it," Kitrina agreed. "Then . . when he was . . staying here he . . d . died and . . Mama died too."

She was silent for a moment before she said:

"But . . however . . beautiful it is I feel it is . . unlucky . . and I am glad you are going to . . sell it for me."

"That is what I intend to do," the Marquis replied, "but as we are leaving in such a hurry, I think it only right to see if there is anything here belonging to your mother which you would like to keep."

Kitrina moved a little closer to him and put her cheek against his shoulder.

"Only you could think like that," she said, "and be so . . considerate and . . understanding. I am sure there will be things of . . Mama's that I have forgotten."

They stopped outside the entrance to the Villa where the servants who were expecting them bowed respectfully.

The Marquis walked in, appreciating the large cool rooms with their white walls, and huge windows looking out onto a flower-filled garden.

He saw, as Kitrina had told him, the places on the walls from which several pictures and mirrors had been stolen, but the furniture that was mostly French was still there.

The Marquis thought that some of the pieces looked very valuable and he thought Kitrina might like to have them in one of his houses in England.

Again he felt himself shy away from the thought of what was waiting for her in England, and the gossip and disapproval of his family.

He had every intention of protecting her as much as possible from the things they would say about her father and mother.

He knew however, that sooner or later he would have to prepare her for the disapproval which could never be completely hidden, and the condemnation they would extend to him for marrying a woman who was illegitimate.

Then suddenly he knew he did not wish to think about it today of all days.

He went from room to room with Kitrina making a quick mental survey of what he thought she should keep and what should be sold locally to the highest bidder.

Then at the end of the Villa there was a room which he himself would have named 'The Garden Room', and which he was sure Kitrina's mother had made very special to herself.

There was a delightful French *secretaire*, a Louis XIV Commode with gilt handles which was obviously very valuable, and two beautiful pictures, a Boucher and a Fragonard.

Looking at them the Marquis realised it would be wise to take them away immediately to the *Sea Lion*.

Kitrina however, was not looking at the pictures, but at the bookcase in which there were a number of books which she recognised as having been her mother's favourites.

Then she gave such a startled cry that the Marquis turned to look at her in surprise.

"What is it?" he asked.

"How could I have forgotten when I came away so hurriedly?" she asked.

"Forgotten what?" he enquired.

"Mama's Scrapbook! I am so glad it is here, and nobody has stolen it, because now I can show you a photograph of her."

She ran from the bookcase towards him with a scrapbook in her hand.

The Marquis sat down on the sofa and Kitrina sat next

to him, pulling off her bonnet as she did so so that she could rest her head against his shoulder.

He put his arm around her and said:

"Do you know, you have been my wife for over half an hour and I have not yet kissed you!"

Kitrina lifted her lips to his.

"Kiss me . . please . . kiss me."

The Marquis pulled her again him and kissed her for a long time. Then he said;

"Let us hurry with what we have to do here, and then we can go back to the yacht. I want to sail away and have you to myself."

"That is . . what I want too."

Kitrina's eyes were shining, her cheeks were flushed and her lips were red from his kisses.

Looking at her, the Marquis thought that no one could look more lovely.

Then as if he forced himself to do so, he picked up the Scrapbook which had fallen to the floor from his knees and said:

"Show me the picture of your mother. Then we will take one or two things from here which should not be left behind, and I will give instructions about all the rest."

"I wish Mama could be . . here today," Kitrina said, "but . . I am sure she . . knows that I am married to the most . . wonderful . . marvellous man in the whole world."

The Marquis kissed the top of her head as she opened the Scrapbook at the end and saw a photograph of her mother in which it was easy to see the resemblance between them.

"You see how lovely Mama was?" Kitrina said. "I shall . . never be as . . beautiful as her."

"That is something on which we disagree," the Marquis said with a smile.

"I wish I had a photograph of . . Papa," Kitrina said, "but Mama made sketches of him and he made sketches of her."

She turned back the pages and the Marquis saw it was

filled with all sorts of souvenirs of their travels.

There were pictures of places they had been to, and Kitrina's mother had made many clever pen-and-pencil sketches of the different native tribes they had met, and of course of her husband and her daughter.

"Now you will see me as a baby," Kitrina said. "Both Papa and Mama drew me . . but I think Mama was the better artist."

She turned the book back to the beginning until the Marquis saw there were whole pages of Kitrina as a little girl, with a camel or riding on a donkey, and some when she was smaller still and was only just able to crawl.

She still had the same angelic little face with large eyes and soft, wavy hair, and he could understand how her mother had treasured every little remembrance of her.

Then Kitrina turned the book to the first page and said:

"Here is the Registration of my birth made in Cairo, which Papa said was very difficult to do because they kept asking where I was actually born. As it was in a tent in the middle of the desert, it was not a very acceptable address!"

She laughed, but the Marquis was staring at something on the same page that was just above it.

For a moment he felt he could not be seeing correctly. Then he said in a strange voice;

"I think that is your father and mother's Marriage Certificate!"

"Yes, it is," Kitrina agreed. "They were married in Cairo, which is why Papa thought it was a good place in which to register my birth."

The Marquis felt it was hard to focus his eyes.

Then he saw that nine months before the date of Kitrina's birth, the marriage had taken place at the English Church in Cairo between Gerald Elke, Bachelor, and Mary Elizabeth Blyton, Widow.

It was signed by the Clergyman who performed the Ceremony and by two witnesses.

He could hardly believe it possible after all the anxiety he had felt.

Then he saw, just above it, a small cutting from a foreign newspaper.

It read:

"DEATHS:
"Blyton, Lord Frederick Montague age sixty-five, at Marienbad on October 22nd 1873, after a short illness."

It was impossible for him to speak.

He just stared at what lay in front of his eyes.

Then he knew that his troubles were over and he supposed that because Lord Blyton had died abroad and the excitement over Gerald's misbehaviour was no longer the sensation it had been, it had never come to his notice.

Now the last problem regarding Kitrina was smoothed away, and he knew he need not be afraid of taking her back to England.

If there were any criticisms of her father's behaviour his relatives would not be so tactless or impertinent as to refer to him in front of her.

She had been born in wedlock, she was entitled to the family name, and no one could possibly dispute the evidence which he now held in his hands.

He shut the book, rose to his feet and pulled Kitrina up beside him.

"I want to look at you on every page of this book," he said. "So my darling, unless there is anything else you want to see in the Villa, I will take you away."

He knew, as she gave a little shudder, that she did not wish to see her mother's room in which she had died, and she said;

"C.can I . . leave you to make all the . . decisions as to what I should keep and what can be left behind? I do not want to . . think about the . . p . past . . but only of the future . . which I know will be very . . very wonderful!"

"That is what I think too," the Marquis said.

He looked at her for a long moment as if he must imprint her beauty on his very soul.

Then he knew that it did not make the slightest

difference to him whether she was legitimate or illegitimate, so long as she was there.

The only thing that concerned him was that nothing should be said or done that would hurt her, and he knew that what he now held in his hand would make her future as wonderful as she expected it to be.

He drew her close against him as he said;

"Have I told you, darling, how much I love you?"

"Not for what seems a . . very long . . time."

"Then I will say it now. I love you with all my heart, my soul and my body, and you are the wife I have been looking for all my life, and never expected to find."

As he spoke he saw the tears come into Kitrina's eyes and asked quickly:

"My precious, what have I said to make you cry?"

"They are . . tears of . . h . happiness," she said. "I . . I have been so afraid since I was left . . alone, but now . . I have you . . and I cannot believe it is . . really . . true."

"I will make you believe that all the dark horrors are past," the Marquis said. "Now we are in the sunshine and we are together, which is more important to me than anything else."

"And to me," Kitrina whispered.

She looked up at him, then suddenly she put her arms around his neck.

"There is . . something I want to . . a . ask you."

"What is it?"

"Will you teach . . me how to . . make you happy . . and show me . . how you . . want to be loved . . so that I do not . . m . make any mistakes?"

"That is quite easy," the Marquis replied. "I just want you to love me, and go on loving me."

"I do love you! I love you so much that you . . fill my whole world," Kitrina said, "but . . suppose I love you so much that you . . become bored?"

The Marquis laughed.

"That is something that can never happen. You cannot love me too much, in fact, I am already complaining because you do not love me enough!"

"How c . can you say anything so . . ." Kitrina began, then realised he was teasing her.

She gave a little choking laugh and hid her face against his shoulder as the Marquis said;

"What I have to teach you – is to love me more and more – so that what you are feeling now is only the beginning."

"That is . . what I want," Kitrina said, "and . . please . . will you start right away?"

The Marquis laughed again, a very tender sound.

Then he kissed her until she felt as if the room was spinning dizzily around them.

The Marquis picked up her bonnet which she had thrown down on the sofa and said:

"Come along, I am going to take you away. The *Sea Lion* is ready to start on a honeymoon which will be the most exciting any two people have ever spent together."

Kitrina gave a little cry of happiness and pulled him towards the door.

As they reached it she realised the Scrapbook had been left behind on the floor.

The Marquis turned back to pick it up.

"We must not forget this," he said. "We are going to enjoy looking through it together, and what is more important, starting a new one of our own."

"Can we do that?" Kitrina asked. "The first thing I will put in it is my Marriage Certificate."

"Of course!" the Marquis agreed.

He thought to himself that they would add the registration of their children so that there would never be any doubt about them in the years ahead.

It seemed extraordinary that one little Scrapbook kept by a loving mother could mean so much to him, and although she was unaware of it, to Kitrina. Yet he knew that what he now carried under his arm was a passport to their happiness in the future.

He took one last look round the pretty Sitting-Room which was arranged, he knew, by a woman who had loved two men in her life, and who had done everything possible to protect her small daughter.

"That is the love that counts," he thought to himself.

He knew that the love he had found with Kitrina was stronger, more perfect and more spiritual than anything he had expected he would ever find.

She was looking up at him with such an expression of radiance on her face that it was impossible for him not to kiss her.

Then with his arm around her he drew her to the door, knowing that their love for each other would grow and expand in the years ahead.

And yet, in a way, nothing could be more perfect than this moment when they belonged to each other as man and wife with no dark clouds to obscure the sunshine.

As if she was a little puzzled by his silence, Kitrina tugged at his hand.

"Let us go back to the *Sea Lion*," she said. "I want to start on our magical, wonderful honeymoon."

"That is what I want too," the Marquis agreed. "Hurry, my darling, so I can teach you to love me more than you do already."

"I . . I am sure that is . . impossible," Kitrina said. "At the same time . . I am willing to . . try!"

She laughed up at him and he laughed back.

Then, hand-in-hand, they went back through the Villa to where their carriage was waiting.

Barbara Cartland
Love is Heaven £1.50

Fane brought his whip down sharply across Delysia's shoulders. She gave a little scream . . . and his lips came down on hers. Taken to a remote castle, Delysia determines to deceive her arrogant captor for as long as possible. As she makes a daring escape she realises that she has lost her heart to a man who she believed hated her, knowing that love could be heaven – or hell.

A Very Unusual Wife £1.50

The reputation of the Marquis of Falcon was such that Queen Victoria would bestow no further honour on him until he was married. His offer for the youngest daughter of the Earl of Warnborough brought him many surprises, not least Elmina's use of karate to repel his unwanted advances on their wedding night. Only when Elmina's life is in danger does the Marquis realise his love for her, and ride like a whirlwind to answer her silent prayers.

You can buy these and other Barbara Cartland books from booksellers and newsagents; or direct from the following address:
CS Department, Pan Books Ltd, PO Box 40, Basingstoke, Hants.
Send purchase price plus 35p for the first book and 15p for each additional book, to allow for postage and packing.
Prices quoted are applicable in the UK.

While every effort is made to keep prices low, it is sometimes necessary to increase prices at short notice. Pan Books reserve the right to show on covers and charge new retail prices which may differ from those advertised in the text or elsewhere.